CHANCING THE FRONTIERSMAN'S HEART

THE WILDERNESS ROMANCE SERIES ~ BOOK 1

ANDREA BYRD

Copyright © 2026 by Andrea Byrd

All rights reserved. No portion of this book may be reproduced or transmitted in any form or by any means - photocopied, shared electronically, scanned, stored in a retrieval system, or other - without the express permission of the publisher. Exceptions will be made for brief quotations used in critical reviews or articles promoting this work.

The characters and events in this fictional work are the product of the author's imagination. Any resemblance to actual people, living or dead, is coincidental.

Unless otherwise indicated, all Scripture quotations are taken from the Holy Bible, King James Version.

Cover design by: Carpe Librum Book Design

ISBN-13: 978-1-963212-63-1

*To the teacher that helped me find my love of writing, Casi Owens.
Without you, I could never be where I am today!*

The voice of him that crieth in the wilderness,
*   Prepare ye the way of the Lord,*
make straight in the desert a highway for our God.
Every valley shall be exalted, and every mountain
*   and hill shall be made low:*
and the crooked shall be made straight, and the
*   rough places plain:*
And the glory of the Lord shall be revealed, and all
*   flesh shall see it together:*
for the mouth of the Lord hath spoken it.

— ISAIAH 40:3-5 KJV

CHAPTER 1

The moon and the stars to rule by night: for his mercy endureth for ever.

— PSALM 136:9

JUNE 25, 1782
RACCOON SPRINGS, KENTUCKY

Jacob stared into the black abyss above, speckled by a multitude of tiny white dots. The full moon off to the right cut through the dark, illuminating the leaves on the trees at the periphery of his vision as they danced in the breeze. As he laid on the hard ground, their rustle filled his ears, along with the chirp of crickets and the croak of a bullfrog. It was an enchanting cacophony...but one that set his nerves on edge. His brain would not quiet on this night.

Over a month on the trail with fifteen other families making the move west, and every day seemed to be the same—breaking camp in the morning and remaking it come afternoon, riding all day in the saddle with only his brothers and mother to converse with and the same few meals over and over. It was growing mundane. And he still had no idea what lay at the end of the trail for him, besides helping his brothers as usual.

It seemed all he was born for. As the youngest male in the family, Jacob constantly followed in the footsteps of his three elder brothers. As a child, it had provided great excitement to tag along on tasks he might not have been allowed to do otherwise. But as they grew older, the choices they made were larger —life-changing, even. First, they all went off to fight in the Revolution. Now, they ventured westward into the wilderness of Kentucky.

While both held their own thrills and challenges, at some point, he had to break free and become a man of his own. Jacob frowned at the dappled sky. There was a time when he had thought to strike off and pursue the life of his dreams with the most enchanting woman he had ever known.

But he was young and naïve. Neither had been old enough to start a life together. Still, that had not stopped him from dreaming of someday. But someday never came. Only the day when she disappeared from his life forever.

Now, Jacob could only pray that when they reached the land granted them for their service, he would finally find a path and purpose. He rolled over onto his side with a huff.

A movement near the trees caught his attention. Jacob rose onto his elbow. Was that a person? The moonlight caught on light-blond hair and slid down the back of a long black garment. The caped woman...

She disappeared into the trees. Jacob's brows pulled together. Why would she go into the woods at night? Perhaps to relieve herself. But after several moments, the woman still had not returned.

Jacob glanced around, but no others stirred. Could she be attempting to run away? It was peculiar that she bore the black cloak at all times, despite the growing heat of summer. The woman kept to herself, never associating with anyone but the family she journeyed with. And the only indication that she was a woman were the navy petticoats that peeked out from under the outer garment and the straw hat with purple ribbon that hid her features. But no matter her circumstances, the forest could not hold the solution. Far too many dangers lurked in waiting.

Jacob slipped from under his cover. He could not leave her to her potential demise, no matter how curious her situation.

After quickly strapping on his pistol and collecting his shot pouch, Jacob strode toward the place where he had lost sight of the woman. A few steps into the underbrush, he paused to allow his eyes time to adjust to the darker surroundings. He examined the ground, but it was nearly impossible to tell which direction she had gone. Still, he searched for each broken twig and ripped leaf, following them into the void while keeping his own direction in mind.

As slowly as he moved, gaining ground on the woman would prove difficult. Jacob stood up straight and closed his eyes. The night chorus continued, but now it was accompanied by the hushed tones of the spring for which the area was so aptly named. Based on the direction he had already traveled, that was where the caped woman was likely headed. Without looking for more tracks, Jacob moved through the trees to Raccoon Spring.

There, in the soft dirt at the water's edge, was a faint set of tracks. Jacob quickened his stride. The trail led back the way the travel party had come from, and he followed it like a hound locked onto a scent.

A shrill squeal split the night air. Jacob stopped in his tracks.

When no other noise followed, he took off in the direction of the sound. His hand went to his side. Jacob released his flintlock pistol from its holster while his mind ran through the potential reasons for such a cry. Besides multiple tribes of Indians, bears and mountain lions roamed the area.

Jacob slowed. That had been a woman's cry, had it not? Not the scream of one of the massive cats that stalked the area? He took a deep breath, his heart pounding in his chest as he ran the sound through his mind again. It most definitely belonged to a woman, one who had been surprised.

Still, Jacob moved ahead at a slower pace. He had best keep his wits about him.

In front of him, the shadows moved. Jacob froze. Slowly, a furry creature took shape as it lumbered through the trees. Moonlight caught on its eyes—flashing green circles on a pointed face. The animal, a raccoon with its ringed tail, meandered by, completely unaware of Jacob's presence. A smile tugged at his mouth. Until he remembered the woman. Had the raccoon been what surprised her so? It had certainly caught him off guard until he could see it better. Still, he had better investigate.

He cut through the next layer of trees and stepped into an open meadow, his shoe breaking a twig. Despite the night noises, it might as well have been a gunshot for how well it rent the air.

Several yards away from Jacob, the woman spun to face him. Moonlight revealed eyes widened with fear, set in a pale face, but he could distinguish no other features before she was moving, running. Into the trees to their right.

"Wait," Jacob called, but she was gone. Leaves danced in her wake, but their sway was the only indication that a person had stood before him. She was not a figment of imagination, though. She was real. With eyes wide like a scared doe. And something...something so familiar. Was it her hair, which had shone as golden as sunshine even in the pale moonlight? Or a particularity of her expression? Jacob's mouth twisted as he tried to force his mind back, to recall the details of that brief encounter.

With more questions than answers, he followed the woman back into the dark woods.

~

*D*awn's heart pounded as she broke through the tree line into the meadow where camp was set up. She stopped and took a deep breath, willing her heart to slow from its deafening pace. First, the raccoon, then the man. Was she not permitted to forage in peace?

She listened, but no sounds came from behind her. She needed to return to her stepparents' location at the far edge of camp before that man found her. Dawn glanced behind her, into the dark forest as she stepped forward. The timbre of the man's voice had seemed so familiar, yet she could not place it. After spending more than a month around the same fifty or so people, though, most everyone's voice sounded vaguely familiar. Still, whomever he was, she could not risk him raising a fuss. Not only would his alert bring attention to her, but her stepfather would see to it that she received extra chores, even on the trail. And, at least for a time, he would keep a closer eye on her, making her foraging more difficult.

But Dawn would not let Mary starve. She could not.

Mary, though her stepsister and no relation by blood, was her charge and the only person she could count as family in the world. Neither of their stepparents wanted them. Besides the free labor the two provided, they were seen as a burden. Dawn scoffed under her breath as she moved through camp as quietly as possible. How anyone could see sweet little Mary as a burden, with her bright blond curls and her big blue eyes, she would never understand. The child was quite angelic, in disposition as well as appearance. So fair and innocent.

Dawn finally found their location in the darkness and knelt where the moonlight filtered over Mary's face. She reached toward the tiny shoulder of the four-year-old but hesitated, for her profile bore such a state of peace, her breaths coming slow and even. They needed to eat their dandelions before anyone awoke, though.

Gently, she gave Mary's little arm a nudge. Then another. After a good shake, blue eyes blinked up at her. Without a word, she offered three of the dandelions. Mary moved into a sitting and accepted them. Dawn held one of hers up before taking a bite. Mary's eyes widened, then she stuffed the whole bloom of the first plant into her mouth.

Together, they sat and consumed their practical feast in silence. Though foraging prospects were minimal at this time of year, dandelions, or *Taraxacum officinale*, were a bounty in their own right. Every inch from the bloom to the root was edible. While it might not be the most delicious of foods, it would keep her and Mary from starving at the hands of their stepparents. At least until they could reach Mary's uncle at Bryan's Station.

Surely, once the man became apprised of their situation, he would take pity on his flesh and blood and remove her from her stepmother's cruel care. Family was everything, and though Dawn had none left, Mary did. The letter in Dawn's pocket, addressed to Mary's deceased father, said so. And Dawn would do all in her power to see her to him. No matter the consequences. Despite how dangerous life at a remote Kentucky station, a small fortified settlement, might prove to be, it was bound to be better than Mary's current circumstances—a practical slave, having to scrounge to have enough to eat to live.

When the dandelions were gone, Dawn gave Mary a smile and ruffled her hair. Then she mouthed "good night" and placed her folded hands beside her head to mimic sleeping. The child nodded and tucked herself back under her cover.

A sound caught Dawn's attention, and she whirled. The man who pursued her had stepped from the woods. Dawn dropped to the ground beside Mary, facing away from him.

Unless he had seen her move, seen her before she ducked down, there should be no way he could distinguish her from anyone else lying asleep. Still, Dawn held her breath and remained stock still. The man's boots crunched across the grass as he drew nearer.

The sound stopped.

Perhaps he was looking around? The steps continued on after a moment, even and strong.

Had he put away his gun? Dawn shuddered. The stranger had appeared as a madman, with wide eyes and a pistol in hand. But then there was a tenderness, a familiarity in his voice when he called to her.

Why had he been so far from camp, though? Had he risen to relieve himself in the night and seen her venturing into the woods? She thought she had been more careful than that. But it was the only sensible explanation. Any other scenario resulted in a man with ill intentions toward her. And despite the fear he had struck in her, it was because of her circumstances, not him.

In her mind's eye, she attempted to paint an image of the man who walked away from her now, his footsteps growing quieter. He was taller than her, though not overly so. Thin but sturdy, with tender brown eyes and dark hair to match. Much like the image she carried in her thoughts of a grown-up version of a boy she once knew. Besides her parents, Jacob had been the one person in the world who accepted her as she was, missing left hand and all. For two short years, they had shared endless adventures exploring the forests and meadows between their homes. Together, they had created memories that sustained her through even the coldest and loneliest of nights. Often, she dreamed of those sweet days as she fell asleep in order to escape the harsh realities of life.

But her and Jacob's escapades had come to an abrupt end the day her father died—the day her life forever changed for the worst. A tear slipped from her eye as she flipped onto her back to stare at the stars above. Why did God have to take so much from her? He created such a beautiful, bountiful world, but why did it seem that death and destruction followed her every step of the way?

Dawn silently released her breath and pushed from the ground so she could return to her own cover. She could not allow herself to fall into that line of thinking again, for it held only heartache. Tomorrow would be a new day and would carry them closer to Bryan's Station. Closer to hope.

CHAPTER 2

The horse is prepared against the day of battle: but safety is of the Lord.

— PROVERBS 21:31

JUNE 26, 1782
BETWEEN RACCOON SPRINGS AND HAZEL PATCH, KENTUCKY

"Did you not sleep well?" Joseph, the middle of the five siblings, reined his bay horse over next to Jacob's gray. Here, where the trail led along the edge of an open meadow filled with tall grasses and wildflowers, there was room for the horses to walk alongside one another.

Jacob raised a brow and slid a glance in Joseph's direction. Was his grogginess that noticeable, or had his brother seen him rise in the night?

No smirk showed on his brother's freckled face. And while Joseph's hat shadowed his gaze, his eyes did not dance with the joy of secret knowledge.

"No. I did not sleep well," Jacob conceded.

"Thought so. You look as though you might doze off and fall off your horse at any moment. Granted, sleep is mighty hard to come by on some nights. At times, it seems the owls are in the branches right above my head and the crickets have crawled up next to my ears, singing their same song over and over."

Jacob smiled. "The owls probably are that close. I saw one swoop between the trees last night." He did not add that it had been in the forest on his way back from chasing the mysterious woman, rather than while lying in their camp.

A chuckle rumbled from his brother all the same. "You know, Jared says we should be on our lands in another week or two. Can you believe it? After over a month of this, we are so close. Tomorrow, we branch off from the trail that leads up to Boonesborough."

There it was—that glint in Joseph's brown eyes over the tipped-up corners of his mouth. Even with the shadows his hat cast, it was unmistakable. His anticipation to reach their land and see what it had in store for them was palpable. A world of possibilities, he had said countless times. If only Jacob agreed.

Instead, he felt much the same as he imagined a man headed for the noose would feel—that there was nothing for him at the end of the trail except for his demise. When they arrived, Jacob would be trapped, living in the shadows of his brothers. He shook his head as though to knock the cobwebs from his head. His future could not be half as horrible as his mind might have him think. "No. I cannot believe it."

Joseph prattled on about the journey and his plans to start a business, but Jacob heard the words without truly listening. The dull murmur met his ears while he ignored the same speech that had been told over and over. One filled with hope and joy.

The image in front of him offered a stark contrast. Riding ahead of them on the trail was the family with the caped woman. Four people, two horses for riding, and two horses carrying their belongings. And although their midday respite was more than an hour done and passed, the same two adults rode the mounts. The same two, it seemed, who always rode. Meanwhile, the caped young woman and a small child, perhaps four or five in age, walked day in and day out. Were they servants? Their sluggish steps and hunched shoulders hinted of a life of drudgery. Did the child belong to the caped woman? Was the sin of bearing a child out of wedlock what caused her to hide away and keep to herself?

Even so, no matter the circumstances, it was not right that they should walk hour upon hour in this heat while the other two rode. Why had Jacob never noticed this injustice? Or never took it to heart as he did now?

If the woman was the couple's servant, he had little right to intervene. But she was a human being. Did she not deserve a measure of respect? Her feet were likely bloodied and blistered by now. The pain the child must be in...so unnecessary when she could easily ride double without putting strain on the horse.

"Just a moment, brother." Jacob excused himself from Joseph's one-sided conversation and rode ahead. After asking his gray for a trot, he easily caught up with the other family. He guided his horse over next to the grass, past the little girl and the caped woman who walked side by side. Then, because the man rode a little ahead of his wife, Jacob was able to come up alongside him. He tipped the brim of his hat in greeting. "Good evening. How are you and your family on this fine day?"

The man slid dark eyes in his direction. "We are well." His tone was even and measured. "And you?"

"Good. Good. Mighty fine weather we are having." Jacob grinned broadly, laying on the cordial hospitality.

"A might bit warm, I would say." Despite the man's words, his voice was as cold as ice. Jacob's smile nearly faltered.

"True enough. But at least we are not plagued by rain." He mustered up some of his brother's optimism. Every time he complained of the heat, Joseph pointed out that it could be raining. And as much as it crawled under Jacob's skin, it was a valid point, for traveling in driving rain was perhaps the least preferable condition of travel they had experienced. Eventually, the continual pelting of water seemed to bore right into a person.

"Yes. I will give you that. Is there some way in which I might help you?"

Now Jacob frowned. Straight to the point. The man did not wish to be bothered, and how could he blame him? "No. No, sir. I only wanted to offer my assistance. I noticed you have fewer mounts than people and thought to offer up my own horse for a time. My legs could use a stretch."

The man eyed him. "We have no need of an additional mount."

Jacob glanced back toward the two who trudged behind the man's wife. Though the woman carefully kept her head down, her ear was cocked in his direction. Meanwhile, the girl watched him with wide blue eyes, as though he held the world in his hands. Jacob took a deep breath at the ache that filled his chest.

"Perhaps the young girl could ride with me, then?"

"She can walk." The man's voice was clipped, his patience having run dry.

"Yes, sir." Jacob pulled his mount to a halt and allowed the family to move on ahead. He watched their retreating backs while waiting for his own family to catch up. Meanwhile, a fiery itch started at the bottom of his feet and slowly worked its way all the way up the back of his neck, as though someone had set those fire ants that lived in Europe loose within his clothing.

Not a bit about the situation set right with him. Jacob clenched his jaw as the caped woman's petticoats swish to and fro with each step, the hem of the outer garment covered in a layer of dust and debris. One way or another, he had to find a way to intervene on her behalf.

~

*D*awn resisted the urge to follow the man with her gaze and instead kept it trained on the brown rump of her stepmother's horse. It was unmistakable, though, that he was the one from the night before. His voice gave him away. When he caught her in the clearing, he only uttered a single word, but it had penetrated the deep, dark night and settled into her mind. There was something unmistakable about it. The timbre. The concern. It warmed a forgotten place within her heart.

But why had he only now approached her stepparents? After more than a month on the trail, being made to walk while they rode. Why did it take a chance encounter for him to be concerned? Then again, why was no one else concerned? Because, so often, people lived in their little worlds, focused only on their own needs and wants.

Dawn bit her lip. Mary's uncle would not be that sort, would he? Connection, though, such as blood ties or a chance encounter, had the power to break through a person's tendency toward selfishness. At least, she prayed it would be so. For he was their only hope.

Dawn stole a glance at Mary. The girl's mouth was crimped and her steps stiff, but she did not utter a word of complaint. The poor child had already learned to take what was dealt her in the two years that their stepparents had been married. 'Twas a shame. Half of Mary's brief life had been spent in servanthood, with no chance to play or be a child. But Dawn was doing her best to see that changed.

Sweat trickled down the sides of Dawn's forehead and

between her bosoms. The humid heat of the day was made worse by the cloak she wore to hide her birth defect. Not only that, but her feet bore blisters and bruises, which protested with each step she took. Still, she breathed in deep breath after deep breath, focusing on the plants and animals around her rather than her discomfort. It was a trick her father had taught her as a young girl.

When snide remarks about the absence of her left hand were made, he instructed her to turn the other cheek and search for another beautiful creation of the Lord's. Though any belief that she was beautiful had died with her parents, her faith in the Lord's handiwork had not. Within nature, one could always find beauty, if they only sought it.

As now, growing at the edge of the forest a few feet in front of her, was a large plant with long white plumes. To most, it was a wild bush to be ignored, but to her it was goat's beard, *Aruncus dioicus*. Dawn smiled to herself, admiring the feather-like flowers, which beckoned for her touch. If only they were not on her left side.

Father had taught her the scientific names for a plethora of plants and animals. Many she had yet to encounter in person, only through books. As a child, the elaborate words spoken in his deep baritone had proved enchanting. Even now, the sound echoed in her mind and brought her comfort. At the time, life had seemed a grand adventure with a world of opportunity waiting at her fingertips.

How wrong she had been.

The distinct sound of horse's hooves trotting up the path behind her pulled Dawn from her musings. Her shoulders squared, and she reached for Mary's hand. She gripped the child's fingers as the hoofbeats slowed to a walk behind her. Had the man from the night before returned again? If so, why? Was it pure concern that propelled him?

"Ahem." The man's throat cleared. "Ma'am."

The warmth in his voice nearly caused her to turn without thinking, but she looked to her stepmother instead. The woman continued to face forward, her back stiff as she rode in the saddle.

"Ma'am...I mean, you, walking here..."

He was speaking to her?

"In the cape..."

Dawn could have found offense in his words were it not for the uncertainty his voice carried. The poor man was simply trying to gain her attention without knowledge of her name. Unfortunately, though, he had gained the attention of all. Both her stepparents halted their horses and turned toward the speaker. Mary glanced up at her, and Dawn gave her hand a reassuring squeeze before she turned.

Her gaze landed on a dappled gray horse with long, dark legs which lent the animal a sense of elegance. Her eyes followed them up to the rider, who wore boots and breeches. Above that was a white linen shirt and a blue waistcoat, but Dawn did not allow her eyes to travel farther up to the man's face. She was a servant, and there might already be repercussions for her simply speaking to the man. Instead, she focused on the third button up. "Yes, sir?"

"I thought you might like to ride for a bit. I could use a walk and wished to offer up the use of my horse." His body moved, giving the impression that he shrugged a shoulder.

"I am sorry, sir. Your offer is kind, but I cannot accept." Dawn swallowed. It was impolite to decline the offer, but she could not risk her stepparents' wrath for a few moments of comfort. It would make it worse when she had to walk again, anyway. She slid a glance toward Mary, who shifted uneasily as she watched the exchange. "But can she ride with you?" Any discipline she faced would be worth it for Mary to experience some relief.

Mary's eyes widened with question.

"Yes. Yes, of course." The gray horse approached Mary, and the man held a hand outstretched. While careful to keep her left arm tucked under her cloak, Dawn looped her right arm under the child's rump to lift her up to where the gentleman could take hold of her.

"Thank you, sir," she said, just loud enough for him to hear, once Mary was settled. He could not possibly understand the magnitude of his simple gesture, but she had to attempt to convey at least a measure of her gratitude. How long had it been since someone had considered her comfort or Mary's?

CHAPTER 3

Because to every purpose there is time and judgment, therefore the misery of man is great upon him.

— *ECCLESIASTES 8:6*

JUNE 27, 1782
HAZEL PATCH, KENTUCKY

Jacob's jaw clenched as he pulled his knife across the piece of wood in his hand, whittling away another sliver to join the countless others at his feet at the base of the tree stump on which he sat. He knew not what the piece would become, but it mattered not. It provided his hands with a productive task while keeping him from trouble. Their camp was set, his mother nearly had dinner prepared, and about fifty feet down the hillside behind the station was the caped woman. While the same couple that had ridden the horses were off at the station house, likely sipping tea and enjoying the latest news of the area alongside Jacob's two middle brothers, the caped woman and the little girl were left to their own devices. Evidently, they were to set up camp and prepare the meal for all four people. And judging by how the little one kept glancing up at the station house, he could almost guess that their tasks were supposed to be completed by the time the couple returned.

Despite his best efforts, Jacob was no closer to knowing the girl's story than he was the day before. When asked a question during their ride, the child would tilt her head thoughtfully. Then she would either give a noncommittal shrug or the question would go unanswered, as though it required pondering, but she lost her train of thought and forgot to answer. In a tiny whisper, she did give her name as Mary, after he had shared his own. Perhaps she was shy around strangers. But it left him more perplexed than ever.

With a loud sigh, Jacob stood and slipped his knife back into its sheath at his waist. At the sudden movement, his mother turned wide brown eyes upon him. "I need to stretch my legs," he muttered. But his gaze never left the cape that swirled and flowed with the woman's every movement.

How could she stand to wear such a garment in this heat? And what was so terrible that she was forced to hide? His steps faltered. Was it truly concern over her family's treatment of her that propelled him forward or simple curiosity? No, it mattered not what the woman hid. She could be with child out of wedlock for all he knew. The girl might well be hers and she a woman of poor scruples who worked as a servant. But none of that mattered. They should not be left to tend to every bit of the work while the couple sat back and enjoyed the journey.

With renewed determination, Jacob charged forward across the grassy meadow. He did not stop until he was within inches of her. The girl, Mary, hesitated before tentatively wrapping her little arms around his legs in a brief hug. "Jacob." Her small voice made it sound as though she were in awe that he stood in their camp.

A gasp sounded, and from where she knelt next to the campfire which she had only just coaxed to life, the caped woman whirled in his direction. Finally, Jacob was able to look her full in the face as she tilted it up to assess the newcomer. Her right hand went to the top of her straw hat as though to keep it positioned atop her head as she slowly stood.

His heart stuttered in his chest as she drew closer and he took in her features. "It *is* you." Jacob breathed the words. His hand extended, then hovered at her elbow, close but not touching. Though her appearance had changed a bit with age, it was her. He knew it. Beneath the cover of her straw hat was hair the color of sunshine and bright sky-blue eyes. Eyes that once saw him better than anyone. Her mouth fell open, but she spoke not a word, likely as shocked as he.

"Jacob!"

At the sound of his name, he tore his gaze from the sight of her and turned. Jonah and Joseph had emerged from the station house and were beckoning him back to their camp. Jacob glanced at Dawn, but her back was already turned, her focus on tending the fire. "We will be fine here." She spoke in a low voice, without looking at him.

He opened his mouth to see that she was sure, but no words came. Instead, a thousand questions whirled in his mind, fighting for space while the woman he had once loved purposefully kept her back turned to him. With a frown, Jacob turned and trudged back up the hillside.

"Well, it is a blessing that we are headed west rather than north," Jonah, the second eldest of the siblings, said as he approached. Of the brothers, he was the one that had most closely resembled their father. Though of a thinner build, he possessed hair as red as the campfire crackling before them and eyes of the same light blue.

Jacob did not have a chance to question before the youngest of the family, their sister, Jemimah, spoke up. "Truly? Why?"

"There have been Indian raids in the area around Boonesborough." Joseph answered for his brother before he plopped down on the grass beside Jared.

"How terrible," their mother whispered. Her thin frame was hunched over the fire as she ladled up bowls of soup.

"We are headed in the other direction." Jared placed his hand on her arm.

"Yes. But no less devastating for those affected." Though she gave him a pointed look, Jared's expression told that he need not be reminded. His jaw was clenched and his eyes dark as he stared into the fire. After being injured in the war, Jacob's eldest brother could stand nothing to do with war or fighting. It had been his idea to travel west, to the land granted them for their service rather than to sell off their shares. Jacob could not blame him. His brother was running from some rather daunting demons.

Thinking of the past, Jacob's gaze slid back to where Dawn and Mary worked to prepare a meal for the two they traveled with. He had a hunch now as to why she wore the cape—she was born without a left hand. Instead, she bore an oddly shaped stump with a miniscule thumb protruding from it. In the time that he knew her, she had never hidden the deformity, and it had never bothered him. Her beauty and her personality were as shining as the sun. What had happened to her in the years between then and now? How had she come to be traveling with that family? What had become of her parents?

"I think you are scowling worse than Jared now." Joseph waved a hand in front of his face and shoved a bowl of soup in his direction.

"Oh." He accepted the bowl and attempted to wipe the sour expression from his face. But questions ate at him.

"What were you doing down there?" In between bites, Joseph motioned to the woman's camp with his spoon.

Jacob cleared his throat and shrugged a shoulder. "Just offering to lend a hand."

His brother seemed to accept the meager explanation, for he nodded an agreement and continued to dig into his food. But his mother's scrutiny bore into him. Her face held no judgment or hint of her thoughts, but she watched him intently. Heat crept up the back of his neck as he attempted to pretend he did not notice. After parenting five children, the eldest of which was twenty-seven and youngest of which was nineteen, it seemed his mother could see right into their thoughts sometimes.

"'Tis good to lend the hand of Christian charity and help those in need." Her voice came out as even and gentle as ever and was accompanied by a tiny, approving nod. Did she truly believe his words? That he had only been doing his part? Or was she simply covering for him in front of his brothers and sister? A look into her brown eyes did not give away the answer.

"Yes." He barely croaked out the answer. For charity was the furthest thing from his mind. Instead, it was how he could get close to the only woman who had ever held his heart and coax some answers from her. Surely, he deserved as much, since she disappeared from his life without a word of explanation. Now, she had reappeared just the same. And in some ways, the way his stomach tumbled, it was as though the years had never passed.

~

Metal clanked against metal as Dawn knelt and gathered the dishes to take down to the creek for washing. Using her right hand, she easily balanced them in the crook of her left arm. Her stomach growled at the sight of the half-eaten ham her stepmother had left on her plate. The woman had been pale as a ghost and barely touched her food when she reemerged from the cabin, but no explanation had been offered thus far, and Dawn knew better than to inquire. She also knew better than to touch the leftover meat until she had disappeared from her stepparents' sight. When she prepared the cured ham for the evening meal, she and Mary were allowed a single small piece for their portion. It was barely more than a few bites, but the consequences were more painful than the hunger pains if she allotted too much to herself or Mary.

"The risk should not be as great to the west, should it?" Their stepmother finally broke her silence with a tiny wisp of a voice.

"No." Her stepfather bit out the answer. "The fighting is to the north."

Dawn paused. What could they mean? They were supposed to be traveling north, to Bryan's Station. She glanced at Mary, who met her gaze but gave nothing away. It would not behoove her to ask, though, so she attempted to cast the thought from her mind and turned toward the creek. But a nagging weight in her middle stopped her after several steps. This journey was all for naught if they were not headed toward Bryan's Station. If they were going west... She had to be sure.

"Are we not headed north?" Her voice cracked with disuse.

Her stepfather cut his eyes at her, then a vicious smile slowly spread across his face. "No. We are not."

Dawn swallowed. "I...I thought we were going to Bryan's Station."

Her stepfather chuckled. A hollow, evil sound. "Yes. Yes, that is what you thought. Melvina was adamant that she wanted her servants to come west with us, so you were told what you needed to hear in order for you to agree to coming." He raised his brows as though to challenge her.

Dawn's mouth hung open. It was all a hoax. There was no Bryan's Station, no hope for her and Mary at the end of the journey. Only a bleak, desolate future serving their stepparents. Dawn's body began to shake. She took a tentative step backward, but the dishes slipped from where she had them perched and went clattering to the ground. Before she could bend to regather them, her stepfather rose with his fists clenched at his sides.

"You imbecile," he raged. "You think you have an ounce of say as to what happens in this household when you cannot even hold on to a few dishes? You should be grateful we even allow you employment as a servant."

Fire crept up the back of Dawn's neck and into her cheeks. Simply knowing where she stood with the man who was supposed to be her stepfather was much different than hearing his words of hatred spewed at her. Never in all her years growing up had she ever imagined she would end up in such a position. Her father had always taught her how to see past her birth defect to her beauty as a daughter of God. Dawn closed her eyes. How could this be her life?

A tear slipped down her cheek. No, she could not give up yet. "What about Mary? What about her uncle?"

"That child is better off to learn what hard work is now. It will give her a purpose, so she can have a future."

Dawn's own fingers curled into a fist. "A future," she scoffed, before she even realized what she was doing.

The next thing she knew, pain seared through the left side of her face and rang through her ears as her stepfather's hand collided with her head. She staggered backward a step and blinked up at his face, contorted with rage. Mary crept up behind her and slipped her tiny hand into hers.

"How dare you—"

A blur of color came from her left and tackled her stepfather to the ground. She and Mary both shuffled backward as the two men rolled over onto the dishes. Despite the flurry of fists and feet before her, Dawn recognized the blue waistcoat from the day before. Only, the blue waistcoat was attached to the face of the man who had offered his assistance earlier that day, a face from her past. "Jacob!"

Jacob had come to her rescue.

CHAPTER 4

Bear ye one another's burdens, and so fulfil the law of Christ.

— GALATIANS 6:2

"Who do you think you are? It is none of your business how I treat my servant!" Blood trickled down from the corner of the other man's mouth, and he wiped it away with his sleeve.

Heat rushed into Jacob's face again. His nails bit into his palms, but he held his ground instead of lunging at the man again. "Servant or not, she is a young woman. And she deserves to be treated as such."

"If it is so much of your concern, then you can have her!" The dark-haired man flung a hand in Dawn's direction. The woman beside him gasped. "She is more trouble than she is worth." He spat on the ground at Dawn's feet, and Jacob struggled to keep his feet firmly on the ground. "And take the girl too."

"Gladly," Jacob ground out. When he turned to Dawn, though, her face was stricken. Tears swam in her eyes. She swayed. He clutched her elbows to steady her, and his closeness seemed to break her from her trance. Her blue eyes lifted from the man behind her to his face before she pulled in a deep breath. Jacob gentled his voice. "Gather your belongings and come with me."

Mary looked on with a sense of wonder, her little eyes wide and round while Dawn went over and fetched a single, small carpetbag before returning to his side. Jacob glanced around. Surely, there was more. The bag did not seem large enough to carry even a change of garments for the two. Was this all their worldly possessions? "Is that all?"

Dawn nodded. Pain flashed in her eyes but was gone in the same second. What had she had to leave behind because of these cruel masters? Jacob's jaw tensed, but he worked to loosen it.

Instead, he placed a hand lightly at the small of her back and guided her up the grassy hill toward his family's camp. His fingers tingled where they came into contact with her linen blouse. It was not exactly proper for him to be touching her so, but he could not bring himself to remove that protective barrier between her and the man who had slapped her.

Perhaps, once he had Dawn settled into camp with his family, he could finally gain some answers about who those people were and what had happened in the years since their parting. He still knew not why she had disappeared from his life without a single word or letter of explanation. What if it was because of something he had done or said? Because she no longer wanted anything to do with him? There had been no quarrel before her disappearance, though. Her smile had been as whimsical as ever as she danced off into the sunset with a promise to meet him at their secret pond the next day.

But the next day, Jacob had waited and waited, until darkness fell. Every day that week, he had waited until dusk, to no avail.

He glanced over at Dawn's profile in the summer sun. Blond tendrils escaped from under the edges of the straw bonnet tied on with a fetching purple ribbon that danced in the wind. Her blue eyes were focused ahead, and her thin pink mouth was crimped with what he could only assume was worry.

Was she not glad to have one another in each other's lives again? Her initial reaction had not exactly been one of joy. Jacob frowned and withdrew his hand. Perhaps he should prepare himself for disappointment. No matter how much the woman beside him resembled the young lady who had captured his heart all those years ago and filled his memories since, the passage of time had changed them both in ways that were not visible to the eye.

'Twas best for him to take each moment as it came and see what God had in store for him. How long had it been since he felt the Maker's hand on his life?

Yet here he was with his past come back to meet him.

Little was clear except for one truth. Dawn and Mary's safety and well-being were of the utmost importance. Answers could wait, at least for the moment. For these two women had fallen to his responsibility. A responsibility he would gladly bear.

As it was, Jacob had his own questions to answer. Back at camp, Jonah and Joseph were on their feet, waiting. All eyes were on him and his guests as they approached. His mother stood to greet them.

"This is Dawn," he said and could not help the smile that spread across his face.

His mother knew all about the woman who had captivated him those years ago.

The elder woman's brows rose, then her eyes widened with realization. "Dawn?"

Jacob nodded.

His mother took Dawn's right hand into both of hers, and her cheeks crinkled in a smile. "It is so very nice to finally meet you."

Jacob's chest swelled as he looked between the two women.

Dawn's cheeks reddened. "Thank you," she whispered. When she glanced in his direction, both her brow and the corners of her mouth were raised. The question of, "You told her about me," was as plain as the blue sky above them.

His mother had already turned her attention to Mary, though. "And you," she added as she bent to take the child's hands into hers in much the same way as she had Dawn's.

"This is Mary. My stepsister," Dawn explained.

Guilt followed the relief that flooded through him. Though his esteem for Dawn had never truly wavered, he never should have questioned or cared whether there was a simple explanation for Mary's presence. It should not have mattered what her relation to Dawn was or, if she was Dawn's child, what the circumstances of her conception were. Not only was every child a gift from God, but Dawn should not be judged by her fellow man on what decisions she may or may not have made.

Jacob should be more like his mother. From the moment they approached, before any explanations had been made, her expression and her demeanor had been welcoming, without even a hint of judgement or question. Now, she knelt and wrapped the little girl, whom she had only just met, in a warm hug. Mary turned wide eyes to Dawn, as though she could not believe what was taking place, before she returned the hug with a smile. Had the poor child never received much affection? She certainly had not in the past month. How long had such treatment occurred? How long had they served those ruthless masters?

"Are you hungry?" His mother asked the question as she withdrew from the hug and straightened. "Or thirsty?"

Dawn held up her right hand. "Oh, we do not wish to impose." She glanced between Jacob and his mother. "I did not mean for any of this to happen."

"Do not worry one bit. God had seen fit to bring you into our lives again, and there is no sense in questioning it." His mother wagged her finger. "Come. Settle in. 'Tis not much, but I made a ham soup with plenty enough to go around."

Dawn's expression was still strained as she lowered onto the ground beside him. But when she took her first bite of soup, her eyes closed, and a look of contentment washed over her. Meanwhile, Mary tucked into her bowl, giving Jacob's brothers a run for their money on how quickly it could be drained of its contents. Was such simple fare a blessing for them? Jacob swallowed the lump that tried to climb up his throat. What horrors had these two faced?

∼

Dawn savored every sip of her soup until the heaviness of Jacob's gaze settled over her. She glanced up from her bowl to find him watching her intently. Heat spread through her cheeks. She lowered her bowl to her lap and looked around. His was not the only attention she had gained. All three of Jacob's brothers, as well as his mother and sister, watched her and Mary with open interest. Though Dawn was accustomed to curious stares, it did not stop her from wishing it was socially acceptable to play dead like an opossum. Although, running and hiding in a burrow like a rabbit should prove to be more effective in her current circumstances.

Yet she was not so lucky as to have those options. No. It was time for her to face the situation in which she had been thrust and to answer the queries awaiting her. Dawn placed her half-eaten bowl of soup on the ground beside her and turned her attention to Jacob. The questions that filled his brown eyes were those of a fourteen-year-old boy who had been abandoned by his best friend without explanation. "Where do I begin?"

Jacob cleared his throat and shifted his booted foot in the trampled-down grass and clover. He glanced at his family and back. "I suppose I should start." He raised his voice as he turned back to their audience. "Everyone, this is Dawn. Once upon a time, she was my best friend. We spent most every afternoon together for two years, fishing and exploring."

"I remember that." One brother spoke up, one with freckles and a shock of red hair. "Jared kept riding you, trying to force the truth out of you because he knew there had to be a girl the way you went around smiling all the time. But you kept to the story that you were going fishing every afternoon."

Dawn's heart plummeted. Jacob had hid her presence in his life from his family? Was he embarrassed of her? He had always seemed so accepting. Though she had kept their escapades a secret as well, for fear that her parents would consider them improper and ban her from seeing him without a chaperone.

Jacob chuckled, interrupting her spiraling thoughts. "Yes, I did. I had no desire to become the family's source of entertainment. I saw how you all harassed Jonah when he was sweet on Jane Wilson, down the lane."

"Aw, that was all in good fun," the same brother protested.

"Yeah, well, just when I was ready to introduce Dawn to you all, she disappeared from my life without an explanation." Jacob's attention turned back to her, his mouth settling into a line. Seven years' worth of guilt bore down on Dawn along with the intensity of the summer sun.

She opened her mouth, then closed it again. She sucked in a breath before beginning again. "My father passed away. I tried to find a way to come to you and explain, but my mother needed me. I...I did not feel I could leave her alone under the circumstances."

"And you could not send word?"

"How?" The two had never divulged the location of their homes. Perhaps she could have sent someone to their meeting place, but it had been a secret shared only between them. How could she break that confidence?

"I know not," Jacob whispered as he gave a slow shake of his head. The pain of their parting was as a wound upon her heart being reopened, and she saw the same reflected in him. Finally, he glanced away, toward where her stepparents' camp sat at the base of the hill. "Who are those people?"

"Our stepparents."

"Stepparents? The man called you his servant." Jacob's voice took on a defensive edge as his gaze snapped back to her.

"My mother married as soon as it was appropriate, for she wanted to secure our future." If only her mother had known what would happen. "However, my stepfather did not believe I should be allowed outdoors, and three years ago, my mother passed away. Without her protection, my stepfather relegated me to a life of service. When he married Mary's stepmother two years ago, she was made to become a servant with me."

"But she is just a child," Jacob's sister protested.

Dawn nodded.

"Why did your stepfather believe you should be kept indoors?" Apprehension laced the voice of the sibling who appeared to be the eldest. Like his brothers, he peered at her from beneath the rim of a hat, but his eyes were a deeper, darker brown than those of the others, almost black. And even through his fiery red beard, she could tell he set his jaw after speaking.

Dawn's shoulders sagged, and she looked at Jacob. No matter how accepting his mother had been or what truths had already been shared, this would be the genuine test of his family's hospitality and tolerance. Jacob gave her an encouraging dip of his chin.

Dawn used her right hand to unclasp the cloak from around her neck, then let both it and her gaze fall to the ground. Multiple gasps sounded, both male and female. She sighed. That was always the reaction.

"Does it hurt?" Another incredulous question from the younger sister.

"Jemimah," Mrs. McFadin scolded gently.

Dawn gave yet another shake of her head. "I was born this way."

"Why did your stepfather hit you?" There was anger in Jacob's voice, but not directed at her. No, he simply wanted the full story. To the point at which he intervened on her behalf and found himself her appointed guardian. Everyone here needed the full story before they decided on how to proceed. And how would they proceed was the question. Though she was out from under her stepfather's thumb, she was no closer to having a way to get Mary to Bryan's Station than she had been an hour ago.

"I learned of his deception, and I...I was disrespectful to him. Mary has an uncle at Bryan's Station, to the north of Boonesborough. We found out about him in a letter that he wrote to Mary's father shortly before his passing. In order to encourage us to come west with them and keep us on as servants, our stepparents told us that we were heading north, to the station. Once we arrived, we were hoping to unite Mary with her uncle. But it was all a lie. As I am sure you well know, we are headed on west, not north. When I learned the truth, I dropped the dishes. He was furious and raged at me, making it seem as though they were doing it all for our future, for our best interest. I scoffed at him and questioned that future."

Dawn kept her gaze fastened to the grass at the toe of

Jacob's boot. She could not bring herself to face him, to face his family, and the judgement that she would surely find there. What if they cast her out as well? All the hope that she had felt at the beginning of the journey now rested in Jacob's hands, and much like a seedling plant, he had the power to pinch it out or nurture it into something beautiful.

CHAPTER 5

The Lord is thy keeper: the Lord is thy shade upon thy right hand.

— PSALM 121:5

The pain shooting up Jacob's jaw alerted him to unclench his teeth. How could anyone treat another human being as Dawn's stepfather had treated her? Her precious spirit had been broken. Even now, she stared at the toe of his boot rather than looking him in the face. All because she had defended herself? "Dawn."

His voice drew her gaze, and his chest tightened at the worry that was written across her face. "You did nothing wrong."

The corners of her mouth lifted slightly, then settled back down into a frown, as though she were unconvinced. Jacob sighed. What could he do to reassure her? To bring an authentic, joyful smile to her winsome face?

"I...I do not know how I will reconnect Mary with her uncle now."

There. That was it. That was what truly worried Dawn. Despite the security and comfort she and Mary would find in his family's love and acceptance should they choose to travel with them, it did not reach to the root of the problem. His family was traveling west, to the same area as her stepparents. But did Jacob have to?

With the experience he gained navigating unknown lands as a scout and messenger, he could escort Dawn and Mary north to Bryan's Station. It was the perfect opportunity for him to blaze his own path. If there were raids to the north, he could serve on the frontlines rather than simply delivering messages from camp to camp for once, all while protecting Dawn from the danger. Perhaps he could finally make a name for himself and, in the process, win Dawn's heart.

"I shall take you."

Dawn's blue eyes, the same shade as the clear sky above, snapped to his, and her lips parted.

"You shall not!" Jared jumped to his feet.

Jacob rose as well, his fingers coiling into fists at his side. No longer would he let his brothers have influence over his life. "This is not your decision to make."

Their mother rose and held up both hands. "No. This is not Jared's decision. Nor is it entirely yours, Jacob." She inclined her head toward him, giving him the pointed look that only a mother could. "Dawn should hold the final decision. But it is also a decision which should not be made on a whim. You should both thoroughly consider the risks involved. Come, let us take a walk."

"Ma..." Jared started to protest, but their mother shot a look in his direction that could quell even a grown man's tongue.

Then she turned her attention back to Dawn and Jacob. "Dawn, Mary may stay here with Jemimah."

Little Mary looked up to Dawn with a question in those big blue eyes that were only a single shade lighter than Dawn's.

One dip of Dawn's chin was all that was required before she scampered off to join his sister, though. Then he and Dawn followed his mother off over the hillside, away from her stepparents and his brothers and sister, and along the tree line.

The afternoon sun was still high in the sky, beating down on them with enough intensity to cause him to sweat beneath his linen shirt and waistcoat. The shade offered by the leaves overhead would be welcome should their discussion grow lengthy. Hopefully, Dawn would be agreeable to his plan, though, and a decision would be reached directly.

For as long as it took her or his mother to utter a word, though, his confidence waned. 'Twas understandable that his mother would have reservations about her youngest son venturing off into the wilderness alone, but why was Dawn so quiet? A quick glance in her direction revealed nothing.

She stared straight ahead, her arms and her petticoats swinging slightly with each step. The sound of their steps swishing against the grass filled the silence and joined the high-pitched droning of the cicadas.

"Dawn, what do you make of my son's plan?" His mother did not turn toward them when she finally spoke up. Instead, she continued ahead of them in her even steps, as though they were simply out for a saunter on a Sunday evening.

Dawn slipped a glance at Jacob. "I do not wish to impose upon his plans, but, honestly, it would be wonderful if he could escort us."

Jacob stopped and faced her, resisting the urge to take her hand in his. "I have no plans. Besides helping build a homestead upon arrival, I had mapped no part of my future in my mind."

Contrary to the comfort he had hoped the words would offer, a small wrinkle appeared between Dawn's brows. "Will it still be possible for you to build with Jacob's absence?"

His mother gave her a gentle smile. "Of course, my dear. Do

not let concern for the rest of us be a weight upon your decision. This is between you and Jacob. I only wish for the two of you to take time and consider if this is God's will for your lives. Have you thought what impact this might have on your reputation?"

Dawn swallowed, and her cheeks reddened. "I...I assumed my reputation was already ruined with the people traveling with us. When we first started out on our journey, I overheard a conversation. Someone assumed Mary was my illegitimate child. I thought nothing of it, for people tend to think little of me, anyway." Her glance slid down to where her left hand was missing. "My concern is not for myself, though. I only wish to do what is best for Mary, whatever the cost."

An ache spread through Jacob's chest. This was the Dawn he knew and who had captured his interest all those years ago. The kind, caring woman who valued every breath of life God had placed in this world. Someone who would give up any and all to care for those that she loved.

However painful it had been at the time, that was why Dawn had disappeared from his life—to care for her mother in her time of need. And from what it seemed, she had done nothing but give of herself in the years since.

No longer did that have to be the case. Now was the time for him to begin making Dawn's wishes come true. If helping Mary unite with her uncle was what her heart desired, then he would see that it happened. But she should not have to sacrifice her reputation in the process. After all, she already held his heart.

Now, Jacob did capture her thin hand in his. Where the soft, tender flesh of a woman's hand should be was the dry, calloused skin earned through manual labor. His fingers tightened around hers. He may not be able to prevent the need for her to perform such tasks here in the wilderness, but he could help her carry her burdens.

"Dawn, there should be no cost to your reputation. Marry me."

~

*D*awn's mouth dropped open. Had Jacob truly uttered the words she believed he did? His brows were raised, and his chocolate eyes watched, waiting for an answer. Yes. Yes, he must have. But surely, she had heard wrong.

At one time, she dreamed that a matured Jacob McFadin would come find her and sweep her off her feet. But that was all it was—a dream. No matter how wonderful their days of exploring along the banks of the pond and in the meadow had been, it was child's play. The reality was that no one in the world could love her as her parents had. And if Jacob did not see that now, he would eventually.

"Jacob. I...I could not let you do such a thing." She looked down. After withdrawing her hand from the tantalizing sweetness of Jacob's touch, Dawn wrapped her fingers around her other wrist, above the lumpy stump with the odd little finger. Tears swam in her eyes. If only she were whole, she would marry this man in the blink of an eye.

He placed the crook of his finger under her chin and coaxed her gaze to his. His handsome face, so strong and reassuring, was blurred. "You know that I do not care."

Dawn swallowed. There was a time when she would have believed his words, and with all of her heart, she wanted to believe in them even now. But life had proven to her that it simply was not possible. The people that should have cared for her, her own stepparents, had treated her worse than dirt, all because she was born different. "You will care," she whispered.

Jacob shifted, his hands going to his hips. He frowned down at Dawn. Time and silence stretched before them. Finally, he was coming to see.

"Then what if I agree to a marriage in name alone? It would protect your reputation as we travel and meet new people, but once I have you safely settled at Bryan's Station, we can seek an annulment. If you wish." Jacob's lips pressed into a line.

How Dawn's heart ached at the prospect. To be married to the man whom she had dreamed of through the years, but for it not to be a true marriage. To know that it was all a ruse that would end at the end of the road. How could she bear it? In ways, this seemed worse than if they married and had a chance at happiness before Jacob came to realize that he could not love her. At least there would have been hope in it, and they would have had a real shot at the kind of love her parents had.

Perhaps it was best for her to face the disappointment up front, though, rather than to fall completely and unequivocally in love only to have her heart broken.

Yes, this would be safer, and she could face it. She would have to. For Mary's sake.

Dawn pulled herself to her full height, which brought her up to Jacob's chin, and met his gaze. "I will agree to your proposal."

Jacob's brows shot upward, toward his brown hat, and a grin stretched across his face. "You will?"

Though unexpected, his joy was infectious, and Dawn could not help the smile that lifted the corners of her mouth as she said, "Yes. I will."

Jacob let out a whoop and grabbed her around the waist, then swung her in a circle. When he settled her back on the ground, she swayed. His bliss was as unbalancing as the dizziness. Why was he so overjoyed when he only wanted a marriage in name alone?

Jacob glanced around, and she followed his gaze. Sometime during the conversation, his mother had slipped away, allowing them a brief moment alone to make their decision. How considerate of her.

Yet now, Jacob turned and tucked Dawn's right hand into the crook of his elbow as he charged back up the hill toward where his mother had rejoined their family. He took great, ground-covering steps that left Dawn doing a kind of discombobulated run as she attempted to keep up, a smile still plastered to her face. She had forgotten what kind of adventure life with Jacob could be. And for the first time since her father passed, she felt a bit of that young, carefree girl still inside of her. A giggle escaped as she quickened her pace, her hand gripping Jacob's strong arm through his linen shirt.

"She agreed to marry me," he crowed as they drew near.

Everyone jumped to their feet, but the reactions were mixed, which helped to tame Dawn's own excitement.

Jacob's mother had a sweet, gentle smile and tears in her eyes as she clasped her hands together and brought them up to rest her chin on them. It was clear that she was happy for their union while sad to see her son leave the fold.

Jacob's sister exclaimed, "What?"

His two middle brothers held similar expressions, their mouths hanging open. The redhead recovered quicker, his shocked expression transforming into elation as a broad smile took over his face. "Congratulations, Jacob!"

He came over and clasped his brother's hand before pulling him into a hug, in which he clapped Jacob hard on the back. Dawn took the opportunity to slip free and stood back, her eyes drifting to the older brother, whose glare could nearly spark a fire. Was it the fact that Jacob would be going against his wishes, the hasty union, or her that angered him so? Perhaps all three.

Dawn ignored his disapproval and moved her attention on to Mary, who was headed her way. She knelt down to the child's level. "You really gettin' married?"

She nodded, mustering up another smile, which Mary

answered with a tiny one of her own. Best for her to believe this was a good change, so that she would not worry. Evidently, it worked, for Mary threw her arms around Dawn's neck. Dawn wrapped her arms around her thin chest and closed her eyes as she hugged her tightly, soaking in the moment. Mary was as close as one could be without being a blood relative, and up until now, Dawn was the only one with the privilege of watching her grow and learn. No matter if she was able to reunite her with her uncle, Mary would always hold a special place within her heart.

Dawn squeezed tighter. What would she do if Mary's uncle did not allow her to continue to have a close relationship with the girl? Life without her was unimaginable.

"Dawn, you 'queeze me," Mary squeaked out.

She released her hold and settled back on her heels. "Sorry, sweetheart." Her own voice cracked as she attempted to swallow down the lump that had formed in her throat.

"Is all well?" Jacob came over and lowered himself to his knees as he glanced between them.

"Yes. Of course it is." Dawn sent him a reassuring smile.

"Mary, do you think you can handle having me around while we go to find your uncle?"

Mary nodded, her curls bouncing, then flung herself around Jacob's neck. Jacob nearly fell backward but caught himself with one hand, chuckling. The sight almost brought tears to Dawn's eyes all over again.

This incredible man was giving up his own family and tying himself to her, a deformed woman with a child in tow, all to help them on their journey. She could not begin to doubt the plan now.

After all, no one could love Mary as blood family could.

But then again, could a man who had not seen the child in more than two years possibly love her as much as Dawn did?

When she was the one who had watched Mary struggle to learn to speak? And nursed her back to health when she fell ill?

Dawn could only hope and pray so. For no matter how sweet the scene before her was, it was all an illusion. The three of them would never be a family.

CHAPTER 6

And they twain shall be one flesh: so then they are no more twain, but one flesh.

— MARK 10:8

June 28, 1782

"What therefore God hath joined together, let no man put asunder."

Dawn swallowed as the man of the cloth, dressed in his somber black attire, finished reading the eighth and ninth verses of the chapter of Mark. Jacob had offered the option of an annulment at the end of their journey, but that was not God's intent. He intended for married couples to stick by one another's side through all—good or bad, thick or thin. Should they truly continue with this if they did not intend to treat their union in the way the Bible laid out? Dawn clenched her jaw and flitted a glance up at Jacob's face.

Just as they had been all morning, his lips were curved upward in a smile. Since the moment he awoke, he had seemed overjoyed to be yoking himself in marriage to her. Was it because he knew there was a way out at the end or because he was truly glad to marry her? Her heart yearned for the latter to be true, but her mind found it folly to believe such. Even if he wanted to marry her now, how long before he changed his mind? Before he discovered that she was a burden, a disgrace. What would become of them then? Dawn swallowed again.

Jacob met her gaze. What had the preacher been saying? Her husband-to-be gave a slight nod of his head as his smile stretched wider. "I do."

Dawn's heart hammered against the inside of her rib. Jacob had done his part. Now all she had to do was utter those same two little words and they would be wedded. The preacher droned on about for richer or for poorer and in sickness and in health. There was no doubt she would stand by Jacob's side no matter what came. The truth washed over her then, and she stood a bit taller. Dawn could not control if Jacob chose to walk away from her, but she could uphold the promises made in her own vows. She would remain true to her marriage for as long as possible and hold onto the tiny sliver of hope that Jacob did the same. They may never have the same kind of romantic relationship some couples had, but many marriages were founded on the need for a partnership. Theirs would be no different.

The preacher stopped and waited. Waited for her. Dawn looked from him to Jacob, and the corners of her own mouth lifted. Jacob was most handsome when he smiled. And there was something about his smile that set her further at ease, as it always had. This was the man who had once been her closest friend and confidant. In whom she had already trusted her heart once before. "I do." She repeated the words he had spoken moments before.

"I now pronounce you man and wife. I hope you both have a blessed life with one another." The man gave each of them a nod before he turned and headed down the hill to join the long line of people and horses which were gathering together to begin the next leg of the journey westward.

No travel plans had been interrupted for their impromptu wedding, but the preacher had graciously agreed to perform a hasty union before the travel party set out once more.

Jacob stepped closer, and her gaze returned to his face. Did he intend to kiss her? Many couples shared a first kiss once their union was complete. But would they? Should they? Their marriage was supposed to be in name alone.

One harmless little kiss could not hurt, though, could it? Jacob's smile had waned, and he, too, seemed to be at war with himself. He glanced from her to his family, who all looked on with eager eyes—beside Jared, who stood with arms crossed and glared from beneath his hat.

Perhaps a kiss at this moment would be improper.

Jacob must have agreed, for he put a hand at the small of her back and guided her toward his family. Mary darted from her place beside his sister and into Dawn's arms. "Yay," she cheered. Dawn gave her a tight squeeze before she lifted her up onto her hip. Then Jacob's mother came forward and embraced each of them in turn. Tears ran down her cheeks, but her smile was steadfastly in place.

Joseph took his turn next. "Welcome to the family, sis." He beamed as he stepped back from hugging her and Mary, and Dawn's cheeks heated. Thankfully, Jonah and Jemimah moved forward to take their own turns. There would be no long, drawn-out celebration rejoicing over their union, for Jacob's family could not be left behind. And the travel party would not wait.

She, Mary, and Jacob were the only ones who would deviate from the original plans.

As soon as the congratulatory hugs were given, the tearful goodbyes began for Jacob and his family. Dawn's gut wrenched as he embraced his mother again, so much smaller in stature and build. If it were not for the three other brothers which would still be at her side, there would be no way Dawn could take Jacob from her.

His mother released him and approached Dawn for another hug. "Take good care of him," she whispered in Dawn's ear. The imaginary knife in her middle twisted. Once again, she was being called upon to fulfill her wifely duties, no matter the nature of their marriage or whether it would last.

"I will," she agreed.

As his family mounted their horses and rode down the hillside to join the others, Jacob came alongside her and placed an arm around her. Bright, warm sunlight spread over the valley before them, and a gentle summer breeze whispered through the tall grasses, making it seem as though nature applauded their union. Perhaps God had a plan for their marriage, after all.

CHAPTER 7

As the lily among thorns, so is my love among the daughters.

— SONG OF SOLOMON 2:2

*D*awn's laugh was a wonderful, whimsical sound that lightened the burden on one's heart and set the corners of their mouth on an upward turn. Jacob could attest to that. Once they had eaten and rested a moment for their midday respite, he had ventured over to inform her that they needed to be on their way in order to make the river crossing before nightfall. Instead, he found himself knelt behind Dawn and Mary as they watched a yellow-and-black butterfly flutter from flower to flower.

"It is an Eastern Tiger Swallowtail, or *Papilio glaucaus*." Dawn's smile came easily, like the morning sun, as she spoke in a hushed, reverent tone. "And those tiny pink blooms are those of the swamp milkweed, or *Asclepias incarnata*. Milkweed, especially swamp milkweed, is where Monarch butterflies lay their eggs."

Despite the lack of blood relation, Mary looked on with the same demeanor of delight. To an outsider, Dawn would appear to be a young mother sharing her passion for nature with her daughter. Both with blue eyes dancing with joy. It warmed Jacob's heart.

Dawn must have noticed his presence, though, for she stood and clasped her hands together. "But I suppose it is time for us to head on our way. More adventures to be had."

Mary turned and rushed to him, arms in the air. Jacob scooped her up and settled her miniscule body on his hip. The poor child was as light as a feather, with each of her ribs palpable to the touch. But he did not mind how her bones poked into his side, for it brought a smile to her face to be carried. Her little soul was so full of love ready to be given away, if only anyone besides Dawn had ever taken the time to let her in.

He would never understand how her stepparents could have ever been so cruel to anyone, much less an innocent child such as she.

Jacob carried her over to where his horse was tied to a low-hanging branch, then waited for Dawn to mount. Instead, his new wife held out her arms to take Mary. "You should take a turn." She inclined her head toward the saddle.

He shook his head. "I could never ride while my wife walks."

Dawn's mouth crimped downward in a frown, and her gaze slid toward the horse. Finally, after her frown deepened, she climbed up. Jacob handed Mary to her, then went through his mental checklist to verify all items were gathered and secure. But even as he started forward along what once had only been a game trail, Dawn's face continued to show her displeasure. How could he have upset her so simply by putting her well-being before his own? Was that not what a husband, what a gentleman should do? Perhaps being married to his childhood sweetheart would be more complicated than he had imagined. After all, who was privy to the intricacies of a woman's mind?

After more than an hour of walking in silence, though, Jacob could stand no more. Throughout the morning, at least Dawn had periodically pointed out various flowers and wildlife to Mary, of which there was an abundance in Kentucky. But since their respite, she had said not a word. Not when Samson scared a pair of mourning doves from the undergrowth or when a bright red cardinal sat chirping at them on a branch overhead. Even now, several yards ahead on the trail, two squirrels chased one another down the length of a branch, causing the branch to bounce and the leaves to rustle, but she seemed not to notice.

Jacob stopped, and Samson came alongside him, halting when their shoulders were in line with one another. When he looked to Dawn, her brows were raised in a question, but no word or sound came from her mouth. He motioned to the tree with the squirrels.

After a moment, the furry creatures came scampering down the tree and around its trunk, one chasing after the other. Both Dawn and Mary gasped. The squirrels froze in place at the unexpected sound, then resumed their play when no danger presented itself. Around and around they went, their bushy tails flickering this way, then that. Then, as quickly as they had appeared, they disappeared back up into the cover of the broad green leaves. "Gray squirrels," Dawn chuckled. "*Sciurus carolinensis.*"

"They play." Mary giggled.

Dawn grinned. "Yes. They are quite playful. I have always enjoyed watching them most in the early spring, before all the leaves come out. Then you can see them bouncing from branch to branch and tree to tree."

"Me see?"

"Yes, my dear. Hopefully, you can see for yourself come springtime."

Pain gripped Jacob's chest. Had the two really been relegated to the indoors for two straight years? Did Mary not remember what it was like to see squirrels play? He met Dawn's gaze over the girl's blond curls. Her mouth crimped, and for the first time since their reunion, reality struck him. Dawn's fair complexion was so pale as to be concerning. No longer did her cheeks carry the sun-kissed look of girlhood, and dark circles rimmed under her eyes.

His precious Dawn, who so loved nature, stuck indoors. Without thought, he moved closer and enclosed her hand in his, giving it a gentle squeeze. A soft smile was his reward, and reward enough it was.

He turned his attention to Mary. "Of course you will. Come spring, we will see to it that you see many a squirrel playing."

As they continued on their course, Jacob remembered that he might not have control over such matters if Mary were to become her uncle's ward. That was the mission, after all—to reunite the child with her blood relative.

An odd feeling worked its way through Jacob's middle. The kind of sensation that, as a scout, would have stopped him in his tracks and made him take cover until he could assess the situation. Normally, it was an indication that all was not right.

Jacob scanned all around as he treaded carefully along the trail, but not a sound was out of place from nature's peaceful rhythm. No movement drew his eye. There was no eerie silence or bird chirp that sounded as though it came from human lips. No, this sensation had nothing to do with their surroundings. It had all to do with Bryan's Station. And what laid in wait for them there.

∼

Mary's body grew heavier where she sagged backward against Dawn, and her little chin nodded downward. Dawn grinned to herself. Though the journey was still difficult for such a small one, it was a blessing to see her able to rest while they traveled. Jacob had seen to it that their meal portions had increased as well, so Mary's strength should grow day by day. In fact, the horse they rode upon was so laden with supplies for their week-long trip that Dawn had to tamp down her guilt at riding double on the animal. But the horse was tall and well-built, with strong bones and thick muscles. Another blessing the Lord had provided in their lives.

While the gentle rhythm of Samson's steps rocked them, Dawn allowed her gaze to settle on the man that walked alongside the beautiful gray steed.

In many ways, she had yet to wrap her mind around the fact that she was married to her childhood sweetheart, to the man who had occupied her dreams throughout the years. On the other hand, it was as though she was married to a perfect stranger.

As much as Jacob's appearance had changed with age, so had his demeanor. In one sense, it was disconcerting, but in another, it gave them an additional point of connection. For she understood his cautiousness. Evidently, life had taught each of them that they could no longer be the carefree children of youth.

Thankfully, though, it seemed they both shared the desire to allow Mary the joy of a carefree childhood. Such was a privilege Mary had not known before.

But now? The sense of wonder upon her face as she watched the butterfly and her bubbling joy at seeing the squirrels were infectious.

Dawn smiled a secret grin at her husband's back. When he

had stopped to point out the squirrels, she had feared that he had sensed danger. Instead, he had given her a glimpse of his old self, of the boy she once knew and who understood her so well. It revealed the kind, caring nature at Jacob's core that had stayed with him through the years.

It was such a difference from what she and Mary had been living with, she almost did not know how to accept it. But she could not be more thankful for it either. How could she have ever lived with a husband who was not kind? It would have been no better than the life she left behind. And even if their marriage was nothing but in name and convenience, at least she had a kind companion to share her life with. And a handsome one, at that.

Once upon a time, she might have believed Jacob genuinely wanted to marry her. But life had changed them, and surely, he was wiser now. Wise enough not to choose a wife with a missing hand. Though he still seemed to look over that feature so easily.

Guilt gnawed at her insides, twisting with each step Samson took. What had Jacob given up in order to take them to Bryan's Station? "Jacob?"

He glanced her way, his brown brows raised under his hat.

"What brought you west?"

His gaze turned back to the trail as they continued walking, and he shrugged a shoulder. "The whole family came. All of us boys served in the War of Independence, so we were each granted land for our service. Those lands are where the rest of my family is headed."

Dawn bit her lip. "I am sorry we took you away from your plans."

Jacob stopped the horse and came alongside her, his expression earnest. "Do not be. They were not my plans. Sure, part of the land is mine. But I had no plans for my life once we arrived. I would much rather accompany you and Mary.

Anyway, it seems there may be some need for soldiers where we are headed." Jacob grinned and shot a wink her direction before turning back to the trail.

Dawn nodded, but she did not return his smile as they continued on. Was this one way in which time had changed her sweet Jacob? He had always borne a sense of justice, but had that grown into a desire to go in search of a fight? Had his time in the war created a need in him to continue fighting the way a winning hand at a game of cards could lead a man to lose his life's fortune seeking that sensation once again? Perhaps she misunderstood his intentions.

Maybe it was time she sought to understand who her husband had been in the years they were apart. "You fought in the revolution?"

Another shrug. "I was just a messenger."

"Really?"

"Yes. I did some scouting, but for the most part, I rode messages from camp to camp." He turned and shot a quick grin at the horse upon which she and Mary rode. "Samson has carried me all over this country. Keeping him was another award for my service."

"Oh. Samson is splendid." With Mary asleep on her, she could not reach to rub his withers, but she fingered the black mane near the reins. The image in her mind of Jacob as an accomplished horseman, riding this majestic steed over hills and through hollers, was an attractive one. "And I am sure that was very important work. Many situations would have ended quite differently if certain messages had not been delivered in time."

Jacob seemed to stand a bit taller then, but he did not reply immediately. "I suppose," he said at length.

Had he never considered his importance in the war before? She frowned. That did not explain his desire to fight the Indians, though. Was it because he had not seen battle in the War of Independence? Did he feel less than the others? After all, his own brother had been severely injured and bore scars both inside and out. And...what of his father? How had she yet to ask about his absence?

"Jacob...what happened to your father?"

Jacob stopped and sighed. He turned toward her. "He was killed in the war. It was his idea to join up. Ma did not want him to, especially when all of us boys wanted to follow him into battle." His jaw worked. "He wanted me to stay home with Ma and Jemimah. But he said he needed to fight for what was right. And if it was right for him, then it was right for the rest of us too." His fists clenched at his sides.

Dawn squeezed her legs against Samson's sides to ask him to step forward. The well-trained animal did as he was asked without hesitation. Once he was beside Jacob, he nuzzled his shoulder with his muzzle, blowing out loud, puffing breaths. Jacob's shoulders relaxed a bit, and his face softened. He brought a hand up to rub under the horse's chin.

This soft, caring side was the one that had always appealed to her most. But his sense of justice was what had cemented their friendship from day one. Jacob had found her crying in the meadow after Billy Johnson had made fun of her at school one day. Without fear, hesitation, or disgust, Jacob had comforted her and threatened to find the kid and beat him up.

After the two of them had shared a laugh, he had attempted to show her how to fish. When her soft heart could not bear the sight of the innocent fish hanging from the hook, he had set aside his pole and followed her along the shore as she pointed out minnows and dragonflies and shared the name of every wildflower growing on the banks of the pond. Besides her parents, it was the first time she had ever encountered someone whom she could be herself around and see complete acceptance reflected in their face.

"I am sorry for your loss, Jacob. I know what it is to lose a father. But do not let his words discourage you. Your role was vital to our victory in the War of Independence."

One side of his mouth lifted in an obviously halfhearted smile. "I am sure." With that, he turned and continued down the trail.

Dawn frowned at her husband's retreating back. Had his confidence been so rocked by his lack of proving himself in battle that he still felt the need to do so? Perhaps there was no future for them, after all, if he was going to leave her to chase after some fulfillment only fighting would offer.

CHAPTER 8

> There is a river, the streams whereof shall make
> glad the city of God, the holy place of the
> tabernacles of the most High.
>
> *— PSALM 46:4*

Despite Jacob having kept a close eye on the map, the Rockcastle River came up out of nowhere. The quiet gurgle of its waters could barely be heard over the rustle of leaves and breaking of twigs as they made their way down the hillside, through the thick underbrush. But in the next second, Jacob's boot had settled into the sandbar at the river's edge. "Whoa," he called to Samson, halting the horse while he was still on solid ground.

"Mary, my dear, it is time to wake up." Dawn caressed the child's pale cheek. Blue eyes blinked open, then her little hand came up to rub at sleepy eyes. She sat up taller and looked around, blinking a couple more times as her eyes adjusted to the afternoon light spilling into the opening where the river cut a jagged path through the trees.

"Where are we?"

"Rockcastle River," Dawn answered. "'Tis time for us to dismount and make the crossing." She handed the child down, and Jacob settled her in the clearest spot he could find before turning back to Dawn. His capable wife was already on the ground and at his side, though. Naturally, his hand went to her elbow.

"I need no assistance." She reminded him with raised brows. But the corners of her mouth were raised ever so slightly.

"I am well aware." He gave her his own grin. Dawn had proven to him years ago that she was capable of most anything she set her mind to. Jacob lowered his right hand to where her left one was absent and wrapped his fingers around the stub at the end of her arm, his thumb stroking the inside of her wrist.

Dawn's lips parted in shock, and her sky-blue eyes widened. Jacob froze. Had he made a mistake in showing that minor act of intimacy when they had agreed to a marriage in name alone? But Dawn did not pull away. Instead, her gaze searched his face. Before he could discern her reaction, a rustle to his right drew his attention.

Silent as could be, Mary wandered toward the river's edge in a spot where the earth simply gave straight away to the moving water in a short drop-off. Jacob abandoned Samson's reins, leaving the animal to his training, and rushed to her. He scooped her up into his arms before she could slip into the murky depths. "Whoa, there, sweet one. Not without an adult."

When he returned her to Dawn, she gave Mary one of those gentle glares that his mother had often given him in his youth when he did something he knew better than to have done. "Mary, you know not to venture away, especially near the river. It could sweep you away."

The little one's face fell, but she reached for Dawn. "Me sorry."

Dawn ruffled her soft, white-blond curls as she held her close. Her attention returned to him, though. "How should we cross?"

Jacob moved aside so she could step up beside him even as he took up Samson's reins. "There is a low spot there." He pointed to where the ripples in the water were more pronounced. "It appears we should be able to walk right across. I would still feel better if I made a pass at it first to see where the deep spots and pitfalls are before leading Samson across. Then I can guide you and Mary."

Now Dawn's motherly glare was pointed at him. "There is no sense in you crossing three times. If you wish to scout it out before taking Samson across, I understand. He is much heavier and could sink into the sand and mud. But Mary and I can follow when you cross back over. It is not as though we are not accustomed to river crossings, and this one appears much easier than some we have already faced."

Jacob nodded. Her words were not untrue. In their journey westward, they had crossed several rivers, including ones much wider and deeper than this one. "Very well."

Leaving Samson behind with Dawn and Mary, Jacob trekked out onto the sandbar. Thankfully, the sandy soil was rock-strewn and better suited to the horse's weight than what he had anticipated. Still, he would need to check the animal's hooves for small pebbles once they were all safely across. A simple stone could bruise the underside of his hoof.

From there, the crossing was just as Jacob imagined. The river was so shallow in this spot that one could see the river rocks through the water, which never rose above his knees. On the other side, he searched for the safest spot to guide Samson and the women up and out, quickly locating the game trail which deer likely used for coming down for a drink of water.

Within minutes, he was back through the cool water and at Dawn's side. "Ready?"

When she dipped her chin, he took Samson's reins from her. While he would still feel better if she allowed him to take the horse across and come back for her, if she and Mary were to slip, at least the water was not deep enough or swift enough to pose a serious danger.

As Jacob led Samson across, Dawn followed along behind the animal. She lowered Mary to the ground and allowed her to walk alongside her but kept a tight grip on her hand. The water would likely come to the child's waist, but on such a hot day, it would likely feel refreshing rather than overwhelming.

On the other side, the three of them crowded into the trees, for the earth immediately began to climb toward a ridgeline above them. "We will make camp at the top of the ridge. 'Twill be best if you and Mary can hike it on your own since it is so steep. Samson is sure-footed, but accidents happen."

Dawn nodded, but her attention was affixed ahead of him as she scanned the hillside for herself. Jacob proceeded slowly, picking his way up the ridge with his horse and the women following behind. For once in his life, he was responsible for more lives than his own, and he had to admit, it felt good. Sure, as a scout, there were lives at stake if he did not deliver messages in time. Dawn had helped remind him of that. But to be immediately responsible for those in his care, it carried with it a sense of purpose. And to be the one calling the shots and making the decisions, even if he considered Dawn's opinion as he did so, it gave a man a sense of pride.

Jacob could not remember the last time he felt as such. Definitely not since they had begun their journey westward. It had simply been an endless blur of following someone else's lead day after day. But here and now, as they scaled the side of a mountain, he was the one doing the leading. And at the end of the day, he would have brought his family through a day's travel all on his own, complete with making the river crossing before nightfall as they had intended.

Of course, there had been no real danger thus far, and the crossing had been a minor one.

Jacob frowned as he positioned his foot upon a rock protruding from the earth and used it as a step. He should not get too far ahead of himself. They were not even a genuine family. Granted, Dawn was his wife, but it had been a marriage of convenience. And Mary was not their daughter.

He could not allow himself to be fooled by the desires of his own heart. He was treading on sinking sand, and it was his own heart at risk of drowning.

~

Despite the heat, the warm vegetable stew made with fresh vegetables from the Hazel Patch station master's garden was a welcome change from their previous meals. The variety of flavors that settled on Dawn's tongue were wonderful.

"Do either of you want this last bit?" Jacob motioned to the pot hanging over the fire.

Dawn shook her head and looked at Mary, but the child had already found a little green inchworm that held her full focus as it crept over a leaf next to where they had made camp. Dawn grinned, delighting in the fact that Mary seemed to love nature as much as she. Though, nature as a whole was quite a new world for the child who had been kept indoors for two years. Every new species they spied was a fresh experience. Which made it all the more fun for Dawn as well.

The soft clink of metal against metal drew her attention. Jacob stood, lifting the pot from its hook. In the other hand, he held their dishes.

Dawn's brows pulled together. "What are you doing?"

He inclined his head down the hill. "I am going to take these down to the river and wash them."

Dawn shot to her feet, her hand and stump going to her waist. "No, you are not. That is my job."

"I do not want you to travel down that steep hillside and back. It is dangerous."

Dawn's cheeks heated. Only an hour ago, she had told Jacob she was capable and he seemed to remember, seemed to understand. Why would he take this from her, then? "I can handle it. After all, it is my place to wash the dishes. Not yours."

"Dawn, we are husband and wife. We are partners and helpmates. I know you are capable, but I also wish to protect you. Let me do this for you. Just this once."

Dawn's gaze slid down the hillside as her jaw worked. While it would be difficult, she had navigated such terrain before. "I do not need protection," she reiterated more forcefully, with a slight lift of her chin.

Jacob's shoulders sagged, and his head tilted to the side. He watched her for a moment, and as he did so, Dawn's ire began to slip. Was it possible he truly wanted to help? Or had they been married less than twenty-four hours and he was already doubting her abilities? Was it simply husbandly concern, or would he continue to undermine her at every turn?

"Why will you not let me do this one thing for you?" Jacob spoke softly, tenderly. The sound reached into a forgotten place in her heart. One that trusted him inexplicably. But it took her back seven years, to when her life had been turned upside down. That was not a place she was ready to explore, for it was a place filled with such pain and loss.

In order to fight the tears that pricked at her eyes, Dawn turned and crossed her arms. She shook her head to let Jacob know he had not won the fight.

Leaves crunched as he crept up behind her. "I will let you do this if you want to. But I just did not want you to fall. *Anyone* could fall."

Dawn closed her eyes. Why was it so hard to allow Jacob to

do this one simple task for her? Was he not correct in that husbands and wives helped one another from time to time? She thought back to her own parents and the love they had shared. Their affection could be seen in the looks that passed between them and the private jokes that only the two of them understood. Even the way they would admonish one another with a smile, as though they did not truly mean it.

But oftentimes, the menial tasks were relegated to the staff. Still, Mother would bring Father his book, or he would bring her a flower. They thought of one another and their needs, their desires. Dawn had always dreamed of such a love growing up. So why did she fight it now when her husband wished to do the same?

She faced Jacob. "Fine. But just this once?" Dawn phrased it as a question so as to root out his true intentions.

Jacob chuckled and shook his head. "Trust me. I am not going to be fighting you over who does the dishes every night."

Dawn smiled at his honesty and relented. "Thank you, then."

Jacob dipped his head in a gentlemanly nod before he started down the hill.

Dawn turned back to Mary. Or, at least, where Mary had been.

Mary was not at the base of the large sycamore tree. And a quick glance around did not reveal her whereabouts. "Mary?"

Dawn attempted to keep her panic tamped down as she walked over and glanced behind the tree. But as she turned in a circle, the familiar little blond curls were nowhere to be seen.

"Mary?!" Her voice rose, and she spun in another circle. Dawn's heart jumped into a speed that rivaled the beating of a hummingbird's wings. "Mary," she screamed again.

Metal clattered, but she ignored the sound as she darted about, looking behind trees. In the blink of an eye, Jacob was back at her side, his gaze searching hers. "I cannot find her. I cannot find Mary," she explained, her voice cracking on the last word.

He gave a nod, his face serious, and then he was gone too. "Mary!" His voice boomed through the forest.

Dawn's head swam, and she could not seem to focus as she glanced this way and then that.

Samson lifted his head and gave a snort from the top of the ridgeline. Dawn whirled in his direction. Jacob must have heard, too, for he took large, lunging steps up the hillside to the animal. "Dawn." He called and motioned for her to follow as he took off down the other side.

She took hold of the front of her petticoats and lifted, then ran after him. She topped the ridge and quickly located Jacob's blue waistcoat in the green woods. Crashing through the dead leaves shrouding the forest floor, she covered the couple yards to his side. That was when her gaze landed upon a scene that would stop any parent's heart in their chest. Dawn froze.

CHAPTER 9

Let a bear robbed of her whelps meet a man, rather than a fool in his folly.

— PROVERBS 17:12

"Do not move or say a word," Jacob cautioned her in a whisper.

"But...but...she is..." Dawn seemed to struggle with his instruction before quieting. He could not blame her. It went against every instinct in his body to stand in place while the child remained in danger. But the danger was lessened for her as long as the mother black bear did not see them as a threat. He swallowed. How long would that be, though? And how swift would her actions be should she deem that Mary or either of them were indeed a threat?

More importantly, could his flintlock pistol stop the bear should she charge? Jacob doubted one single ball would fell the wild animal. Especially if she was in a rage. During the War of Independence, he had heard fantastical stories about men accomplishing feats that seemed impossible for a human, even when mortally wounded. He could only deduce that a bear would be the same. Or even worse.

Still, Mary was several yards away, and the black bears were drawing closer, especially the three cubs which romped ahead of their mother, tumbling and climbing upon one another.

"Mary," he called in as quiet as a voice as she might hear. When she did not answer, he added a bit of urgency. "*Mary.*"

When her little ear turned slightly in his direction, indicating that she had heard, he gave his instruction. "Back slowly toward me."

The smart child gave a dip of her chin without turning to look his way and edged a foot toward the sound of his voice. Better for her lighter footfalls and shorter stature to do the moving than for him. But he would be there in an instant if needed.

Jacob kept an eye on the mother bear without ever losing track of Mary's progress, all the while conscious of his own thundering heart and Dawn's rapid breathing. Just in case, he carefully worked a shot from his shot bag and withdrew his pistol from its holster. He may not have as much experience as the soldiers on the front lines, but he could load the weapon with his eyes closed. He had to be able to. As a messenger, you never knew if the need might arise in the middle of the night or thick of fog.

It may not work, but he had to be ready to get a shot off if things went against his favor. Both then and now.

Somehow, the black bears continued with their march without noticing their movements, likely focused on the water source down the ridge. But that could change at any moment.

Mary kept her steady pace, gradually closing the gap between her and him.

Then her foot snagged on a root. In the blink of an eye, she was on her rump, and a tiny gasp escaped her. Jacob's eyes widened, and his attention darted to the mother black bear.

She stopped and looked toward Mary, sniffing the air. Jacob thought his heart would beat out of his ears as he waited for her reaction.

One black paw moved closer, and Jacob's fingers twitched, itching to grab Mary and run. But the swift movement would only exacerbate the situation.

"God, please, no. Please protect her. Please send the bear away." Despite the quietness of her whispered pleas, Dawn's voice behind him was laced with panic. He could not reprimand her, though, could not tell her not to pray. For what choice did they have? And what other comfort did she have? Thankfully, Mary did not move a muscle after falling and simply stayed put on the ground.

After a bit more sniffing, the mother black bear lumbered off after her progeny.

As soon as the family of bears was out of sight, Jacob holstered his gun and made for Mary. Dawn beat him to her side and wrapped the child in a hug, tears spilling from her eyes. Jacob swallowed and held his ground. It seemed too private of a moment to interrupt.

When Dawn finally loosened her hold, though, Mary turned to him. "Jacob?"

He knelt. "Yes?"

Mary left Dawn's lap and came over to wrap her arms around his neck. "Thank you."

Jacob returned the child's embrace but glanced at Dawn. "I did not do anything."

"Yes, you did," Dawn replied for the child, nodding as tears continued to slip down her cheeks. "You kept your head and kept her safe. We would not have known what to do without you."

They sat there, Dawn looking on and Mary hugging him, with not a care in the world that they were in the middle of the forest. They were simply glad that the danger had passed. After some time, Jacob remembered what he had been doing before Dawn had begun screaming for Mary.

He eased Mary from him and quickly regained his footing. "I need to get those dishes washed. And bury our food stores so as not to attract the bears."

Dawn came to him and placed a hand on his arm. "I can wash easier than I can dig. If you will let me help, we can accomplish both tasks at once."

Jacob frowned as he took in her earnest face with those blue eyes that so easily melted his heart. He did not want her to have to tend to either task, much less to risk putting her life in danger by sending her to the same river where the bear was likely taking a drink with its cubs. But she had a point. Digging would be almost impossible for Dawn. And he knew how much it pained her to admit that.

"Be careful. Watch for the bear and try to stay out of its sight. Remember not to move or make a sound if she does see you. And if she comes toward you or acts aggressively, use the dishes to make loud noises. I will be right here if you need me."

Dawn nodded. "Keep Mary here with you."

Jacob dipped his chin in a nod, but his words stuck in his throat as he realized what she said. He could have bent and kissed her right then, for the pride and joy that washed over him. He was well aware of what a great deal it meant for Dawn to entrust Mary's care to him in the face of danger.

Perhaps his plan was working, after all. By keeping a level head when it was needed most, it seemed he had worked his way into Dawn's trust, and hopefully, into her heart. If he could prove himself worthy, perhaps he could win her affections once more.

And yet, they had still to make it through the night.

June 30, 1782

*R*ocks clattered and water splashed as Jacob stepped into the shallow waters of the wide creek. Beside him, Dawn entered the sunny creek bed with Samson in tow, the animal making a louder clatter as all four hooves came down into the rocky creek. She turned and grinned up at Mary, who sat atop the horse as though she were a princess atop a royal steed, her back straight and tall and the hint of a smile on her face as she took in all around them.

Then Dawn tipped her face upward, blinking at the bright sunlight. She sighed and closed her eyes, simply soaking in the moment. Despite the oppressive heat that had settled in come mid-June, she still relished in the feel of the sun's warmth against her face. For so long, she had been made to do without. One could forget what a blessing the light could be. That was, until they had to face the darkness.

As Jacob sloshed over to a deeper spot to refill their canteens, Dawn shook the dreary thoughts from her mind and instead watched the cold water soak the bottom of her petticoats and swirl around Samson's dark grey legs. Tiny fish darted in and out between the horse's fetlocks before moving on downstream.

When Jacob walked over and offered her the canteen for a drink, her mouth twisted in amusement. While fresh, moving water was not exactly scarce in this land, Jacob seemed to make sure that she and Mary drank more than their share, as though their supply might run out at any minute. Of course, the landscape did change so often, the water was not always available right at the moment it was needed.

Dawn accepted the drink and then handed the canteen up to Mary. With proper nourishment, the little one already seemed to be perking up. Though still pale and thin, there was a warmth and brightness to her face that had been lacking before.

While Mary sipped the water, Dawn returned her attention to her husband's easy smile, to the face that had so quickly become familiar to her again. "I know it will be nearly unbearable on up in the day, but the sun feels so wonderful. It reminds me of those carefree days on the bank of the pond."

"I miss those days as well. There was no pressure. To do anything. Be anything."

Dawn frowned. How much of that pressure had been placed upon his shoulders by her and Mary? Thin lines creased the edges of his eyes and mouth. Were they added by age or by the stresses of life over the past years? Dawn shook her head. "I never meant for any of this to fall upon you, Jacob."

He stepped closer. "You are not a burden, Dawn. This journey is not a burden. I meant what I said. I had no plans, no direction."

Jacob seemed earnest, but how could it be that he truly did not have a single plan for his future? And what of his mother? His siblings? "Still. We have taken you away from your family."

Jacob raised his brows. "Dawn, you know me. Did I ever desire to be around my family rather than spend time with you?"

The air seemed to leave Dawn's lungs, and she blinked up at him. Sure, during those days in the meadow and alongside the pond, they had each seemed drawn to one another as a moth to a flame. Every waking moment not dictated by their parents or other obligations, they had spent in each other's company. But that had been seven years ago, when they were young and carefree. While in some ways it felt as though it was only yesterday, much had occurred in the meantime, and life was much more complicated now. "I...I suppose not. But that was so long ago."

"That fact has not changed, Dawn."

Dawn swallowed. He could not mean all that he implied.

That he felt as strongly about her then as she had always hoped and still did? It could not be. No, it was best not to allow herself to daydream about what deep affection her husband seemed to be declaring. Perhaps the sun beating down upon them had made him delirious? She had to change the subject. Dawn rolled her eyes and forced a laugh. "You make it sound as though your family is insufferable."

Jacob chuckled. "The house does get a little loud and full with the five of us. And you can always count on them to poke at you. But they always mean it in good fun." He shrugged. "I know Jared seemed tough, but he went through a great ordeal in the war. He was caught in an explosion and is lucky to be alive. It has hardened him."

Dawn placed a hand on his arm. "I am sorry. Perhaps time will work to heal the wounds that remain on the inside. We will pray it is so."

"Yes. Thank you." Jacob took a deep breath. "Well, best to head on our way, I suppose."

After they crossed the creek, there was a wide, level trail that traveled alongside the water for as far as the eye could see. For the first time, it seemed, since they had entered Kentucky, it actually appeared that people had come this way before them, the earth bearing the scars of their steps. Of course, to their right, the land drifted up and up, but for now, what a welcome respite.

Even Mary seemed to understand what a blessing it was, for she squirmed atop Samson. "Me walk?"

"Of course you can, my dear." Dawn moved toward her with a grin. As Mary began to slide from the saddle, though, Jacob came to her aid. He whisked her into his arms and spun her around, coaxing from her fits of squealing laughter.

After several times around, Jacob stopped and seemed to take a moment to gather his own bearings. Then he slowly settled Mary on the ground. A broad, toothy grin split her face as her eyes attempted to focus on the trees around them. It took only a moment before she was marching right along beside Dawn, holding the ends of the reins as if she was the one leading the massive animal.

Less than half an hour later, though, the idea of walking had lost its shine. Head down, Mary did not utter a word of complaint. But her feet trudged forward one slow step after another, the toes of her boots dragging in the dirt. Jacob noticed her lackluster attitude and gave Dawn a knowing look. Then he knelt in front of Mary. "How would you like to ride on my shoulders and see how many tree branches you can reach?"

Immediately, both Mary's eyebrows and her spirits lifted, and her toothy grin returned. She nodded emphatically, white-blond curls bouncing. As soon as Jacob turned, she scrambled up onto his shoulders. And as he began walking, her little arm shot into the air, reaching for the branches overhead.

Dawn chuckled and shook her head, but it warmed her heart to see. Despite all her squirming and stretching, Jacob carried her along merrily as could be. Mary had been in need of a father figure for quite some time, and he was the perfect man for the job. At least until they made it to Bryan's Station, that was. She frowned. Would Mary's uncle step into that role as easily as Jacob had?

CHAPTER 10

Come, my beloved, let us go forth into the field;
let us lodge in the villages.

— SONG OF SOLOMON 7:11

July 3, 1782
Between Big Hill and Richmond, Kentucky

"Can you believe that, after all this time in the wilderness, we will have been to two different settlements in a single day?"

Jacob grinned at the bounce in Dawn's step as she spoke. Though she loved nature, she, like anyone else, could not help but be thankful for the conveniences a station or town provided. The company of others was nearly always welcome after such a solitary existence. He could only imagine that sensation was heightened for Dawn, who had such little human interaction for all these years. "It is strange, is it not? And Richmond is the largest town we have seen yet. Likely, the largest we will see."

Her steps faltered now. It was barely noticeable, but there was a slight hesitation before her next step. Her hand went to her other arm. "It has been years since I have been seen inside a town without a cover. We have only seen small stations."

Jacob stopped her with a hand on her arm. "I know your stepparents did not set a good example of how people will react to your difference, but has anyone seen you differently in all the course of our travel?"

Dawn avoided his gaze. "There have been a few."

"True. But your stepparents are two of those. And they treated Mary horribly as well, and there is no physical difference with her."

She closed her eyes, and a pained expression washed over her face. "It is difficult not to doubt. Not to believe the worst."

"I can only imagine." Beside them, the wind blew the tall grasses. Their gentle rustle filled the silence and gave him an idea. "But try to see the light within people as you see the light in the world around you. You have such a gift for that."

That brought a slight lift to the corners of her mouth. Dawn peeked at him with raised brows. "Flowers do not tend to disappoint."

Jacob chuckled. "What about the poisonous ones?"

She returned his laugh with the soft, melodic sound that warmed his heart. "You have a point."

The look she gave him then, as she smiled up at him, uprooted his insides and swirled them around. It took all in his power not to take her into his arms and kiss her. But that was not their agreement. So instead, they turned and continued their journey, with Mary riding astride Samson.

"I will try."

"Good." He nodded. Perhaps it would be good to give Mary a better example of not being suspicious of people's words and actions. She did not deserve to live her entire life jaded by her stepparents' actions.

As they crossed over the rise, the town stretched out before them. Silence fell over their small group as they closed the gap.

Just before they reached the first buildings, a grizzled old man in a crumpled hat and a threadbare waistcoat came walking down the path, leading a donkey behind him. He stopped and removed the hat, which had certainly seen better days, and wiped an arm across his brow before offering them a friendly smile. "Welcome. Have you traveled far?"

"Originally, yes, from North Carolina. But today, we only journeyed from Big Hill. 'Twas quite a simple journey. Is there a place we could lay down our heads for the night?"

"Ah, yes. Yes. Just down that way and around the corner." He pointed in the direction he spoke of.

Jacob nodded and turned to Dawn. "See," he whispered.

She dipped her chin and offered him a small smile, before broadening it for the man with the donkey.

Richmond was as large as the city from whence they originally hailed in North Carolina. It was strange to see such a sprawling settlement in the middle of the wilderness. But here it was. Was that what his own family would help establish one day? Or would they each live quietly, unified with the land? The thought struck from nowhere, and he dashed it from his mind.

Dawn and Mary were his only concerns for now. He would find them a warm meal and a nice place to rest for tonight. Perhaps even a place with a bed. Then he would lead them on to Bryan's Station. Only a couple more days before their journey would be complete.

Jacob nearly stopped in his tracks. Bryan's Station had always been the end goal, but now that it loomed ahead, he was not ready for the journey to end. Not if it meant an annulment. He was not ready for Dawn and Mary to depart from his life.

At once, they found the inn. It was barely more than a home, the small wooden sign beside the door the only feature designating it otherwise. Jacob knocked. The door opened to reveal a plump woman with dark hair and a broad smile on her face. "Welcome. Are you needing a place to stay for the night?" She dried her hands on her apron as she spoke.

"Yes. I was hoping you would have a room for us. This is my wife, Dawn, and our daughter, Mary." He stepped aside and motioned to both of them.

When the woman's gaze landed on the stump at the end of Dawn's arm, her brows raised and her smile vanished. "I apologize. We are all full for the night." She barely had the words out of her mouth before she had shut the door in his face.

Jacob stopped with his own mouth ajar as he stared at the wood boards a few inches from his nose.

When he turned, it was impossible to miss Dawn's deep frown and knitted brow. "All is well. We will find somewhere else." Normally, he might think that a lie, but the town seemed plenty large enough to contain another inn or, at the least, a benevolent stranger. He moved on down the path, toward what seemed to be a town square where several people had carts set up in front of shops. Surely, someone there would have information that would be of assistance.

Jacob approached the first vendor, but when the man spied Dawn, he ducked back behind his cart as though he were searching for some lost item. The next several people they passed seemed quite preoccupied with various tasks of their own. That was, until they reached a stunning flower cart, filled with colorful blooms.

"Good afternoon! Oh, and what do we have here?" The vendor, a woman with a kerchief tied around her hair, grinned down at Mary. "You are such a sweet one. A rose is exactly what you need." She pulled a red rose from her cart and trimmed it down to barely more than two inches of stem, then tucked it behind Mary's ear. "Oh, it suits you perfectly."

The woman was quite different from the other vendors,

different from most women Jacob had ever encountered. Her red curly hair was loose and wild, with only the blue kerchief tying it back from her face. Her clothes were a hodgepodge of various bright colors, her blouse a burnt orange, and her petticoat held alternating layers of deep purple and bright magenta.

She turned to Dawn next. "And one for her mother." She tucked a lovely purple flower behind Dawn's ear that matched the purple ribbon in her straw hat and complemented the flush in her cheeks.

"Oh, I am not…" Dawn began before stopping herself with a glance at him. She had nearly given up their ruse by accident.

Jacob wrapped an arm around her and pulled her close. "She is her stepdaughter," he proffered instead.

The woman's smile had not faded through the entire exchange and did not now either. "You care for her, tending to her every need, do you not? And love her as if she were the fruit of your own womb?"

Dawn nodded.

"Then she is your daughter," she reassured Dawn before she glanced between her and Jacob. "Now, I believe you have a need outside of a couple flowers?"

Jacob blinked, his mind taking a moment to catch up with the shift in conversation. She must have heard them inquiring about lodging. "Well, yes. We were trying to find somewhere we could stay the night. We have been traveling and are well equipped to camp outside the bounds of the town if need be, but I had hoped to find a better place for these two to lay their heads tonight."

"Oh, that shan't be a problem. Come with me." At that, she turned and wheeled her cart down the road. They followed her to a nice little cabin on the edge of town with a shed built onto the left side for firewood. She pushed the cart into the open area beside the wood before issuing further instruction. "There is a small corral in the back where your horse can stay as long as he does not mind the company of my goats."

Jacob chuckled. "I am sure he will not mind." He turned to Dawn. "You will be fine while I tend to Samson?"

Dawn nodded up at him. Jacob resisted the urge to lean in and kiss her, but took her hand in his and gave it a gentle squeeze. Her smile was a sweet reward for the simple gesture. Perhaps there was time yet to win her heart.

~

*D*awn's stomach fluttered as Jacob's hand slipped from hers and he left her with a grin. She sucked in a breath to steady herself before she turned to the kind woman who opened her home to them and took Mary's hand. Growing all around the cabin were flowers of all sizes and colors, including varieties from all over the world. There were some Dawn had never laid eyes upon but had only read about. "Your home is exquisite. How have you managed to grow all of these?"

"My adoptive mother loved flowers. When they moved west, she told her husband she would only come if she could bring her flowers with her. She brought every seed and bulb she could salvage and purchased additional ones, bartering with items from their home they would never need again. Along the journey, she gathered even more. Even so, when we would go foraging, she was always searching and adding."

"Incredible," Dawn breathed, her cheeks aching for how wide she was smiling. They followed the woman into the main room of a cabin that was no different on the inside than the outside. It was filled with little frillies and lace embroidered with colorful flowers. Knitted blankets and shawls were draped over nearly every piece of furniture. Jars of flowers sat on the table and counters and side tables.

The woman must have followed the sweep of Dawn's eye and noted her mouth unabashedly hanging open in awe. "In the winter, I cannot garden and prune, so I need another income, as well as something to do with my hands." She held up her hands for them to see. "God seemed to make me where I cannot sit still for much more than a minute. Even when I pray or read my Bible, I will pace about this floor."

Was talking ceaselessly another quality God blessed her with, or was it simply that she was glad for the company? What a blessing it would be to have this woman's boundless energy.

"I have always found it good to keep busy," Dawn agreed. Though, often, hers had not been by choice. When not forced to by her stepparents, Dawn had sought busyness as a way to distract herself from the pain of her circumstances.

"Are you hungry? Thirsty? Have a seat." The woman gestured toward the table.

"We are well." Dawn pulled out a seat for Mary, then for herself.

"One can always eat." She poured a couple cups of water from a pitcher and set them on the table before them, then went back to the counter where she fetched a partial loaf of bread from the basket and a couple of plates. She cut two slices, placed them on the plates, and handed them over as well. Then she was off again, whirling over to a place in the floorboards where she lifted a hatch. In what must have been a small root cellar, she withdrew another bit of food which she took over to the counter and sliced. When she added it to their plates, Dawn's eyes widened. "Cheese?"

The woman nodded, her smile ever-present. "Goat cheese."

Dawn gingerly picked up the delicacy and placed it atop her bread before taking a bite. She closed her eyes and savored the unexpected and delightful flavor. She had not consumed even the tiniest morsel of cheese in years.

While they waited for Jacob, the woman flitted about,

preparing another plate and cup. "This is just a bit to tide you over until mealtime. I will prepare you a hearty meal this evening to sustain you for your travels tomorrow. You did say you were only staying for the night, correct? Of course, it is perfectly acceptable if you need to stay longer. My home is open to you for as long as you need."

Dawn could not help the chuckle that escaped. "We only have need for the night. Then we will continue on to Bryan's Station."

The woman froze then and turned toward her. This time, the smile was gone from her face. "It is not safe up there."

The joy slipped from Dawn. They had no choice but to go. But how could she explain that without telling the truth, without explaining that they had lied? For the moment, she would simply keep quiet and perhaps, Jacob could lend some support in a moment.

When he cracked the door open and broke the tension that had coiled in his absence, it took a measure of restraint to keep herself from going to him. Instead, she pulled out the chair beside her with a smile. "Mrs..." Suddenly, Dawn realized she had yet to ask the woman's name.

"Jenkins," the woman supplied. "But it is only 'Miss.' I never married."

"Miss Jenkins has prepared some bread and cheese for us."

"Cheese?" His voice held the same awe as hers had.

"Yes. From my goats. Your wife says you are traveling to Bryan's Station?" There was no judgment in the woman's voice, only...fear? Had she lost someone in the Indian raids? Was that the reason for her caution?

"Yes. We are traveling to meet family." Jacob's hand slipped under the table to envelope her stump. It never seemed to bother him to touch it, as though it were as natural as holding her hand. And thankfully, he was also blessed with quick wit. "Oh. Yes. Well, I understand the need to be near family."

She nodded as she continued to concentrate on her task at hand. "It was dangerous for my own parents when they came west. But the tensions are high to the north. There have been attacks. I...I do not mean to scare you or to alter your plans. I only want you to be aware before you head on."

Jacob's grip tightened, as though to reassure her. "We appreciate your caution. But I do believe we will continue with our plans. We cannot begin to express how much we appreciate your hospitality as well. Not everyone was as welcoming."

Miss Jenkins turned to them with her warm smile back in place. "I can imagine so. Many people fear that which is different. That is why I always try to keep an open heart and an open mind, as my mother taught me. And if you still plan to travel on, then I must get to preparing that hearty meal for you."

"Let me help you." Dawn placed her hand atop Jacob's. His skin was so warm and reassuring. She held onto that feeling as she slipped from her seat and went over to the counter to help Miss Jenkins. They would need one another over the next days.

CHAPTER 11

> Then I will give you rain in due season, and the
> land shall yield her increase, and the trees of
> the field shall yield their fruit.
>
> — *LEVITICUS 26:4*

July 4, 1782
Between Richmond and Bryan's Station

"I will be praying for your safe journey," Miss Jenkins called after them, waving from where she stopped at the town's edge. Once the woman had made her caution known, she had stepped back, allowing them to make their own decision. And been the most gracious hostess all the while. Besides their usual belongings, they carried a cloth with a whole loaf of bread and round of cheese for the midday respite. Instead of a small, simple meal, they would have a veritable feast come midday. Then, before the end of the day, they would be at Bryan's Station.

Jacob's joy slipped, and he slid a glance toward Dawn. Did

she dread their arrival as much as he? Or would she be glad to be rid of him if they were granted an annulment? Though it was his idea, he could not imagine actually carrying it out. He had only said the words in the hope of winning her heart before they reached the station, but the journey had gone by so quickly. It had been foolish to believe he could make a difference in such a short span of time, but he had hoped that their shared history would make up for lost time.

But he was not sure that he had gained much ground. Last night, holding her hand and watching her look to him for guidance and support—those were the moments he longed for. But how many more would there be?

Beside him, Dawn sighed. The kind of sigh that slips out when one is stressed or exasperated...or a big decision lies ahead of the person. Should he chance holding her hand now? Of course, he could not actually hold her hand from this side. Not that he minded, but it would be wonderful to feel her fingers slip into his. To feel her returning the embrace. "Here, let me lead Samson for a bit," he offered as he rounded behind her and reached between her and the horse. "You do not mind, do you, Mary?"

Mary grinned and shook her head so that her curls whipped into her face. If anyone had won someone's heart this week, it was Mary who had won his. Already, he could hardly imagine handing her over to this unknown uncle. But the man could not be denied his own kin either. So he flashed a grin at Mary and stepped between her atop the horse and Dawn beside him as she relinquished the reins. Then he caught Dawn's hand. Her hand was so warm and petite in his, such a complementary fit, that it made his chest swell with delight.

When he chanced another glance her way, it was difficult to read her expression. But she did not pull away, so he settled into the comfortable moment. Likely, they would not all be able to walk side by side as they were now once they made it across the meadow. Though, with these areas more settled, the path was more apparent, as though it were traveled regularly.

Above them, a turkey vulture circled, passing in and out of the sunlight even at the early hour. Of all the animals that roamed the beautiful lands of Kentucky, they were one of his least favorite. Due to their scavenging ways, he associated them with death.

Jacob frowned and surveyed the area. They were in an open field with a wind blowing the tall grass this way and that, keeping the morning sun from becoming stifling.

"Is all well?" The skin between Dawn's brows was drawn together in a wrinkle.

Jacob loosened his grip, realizing he had tightened his fingers around hers. He offered her a smile and rubbed his thumb over the soft back of her hand. "Of course."

"'Tis odd, is it not? To think that, after all we have been through, we will be at Bryan's Station before the day's end?" From her tone of voice, he could not discern how she felt about that fact.

"It is," he agreed, keeping his own voice ambivalent.

Dawn took a deep breath. "And we will finally meet Mary's uncle."

"We will."

"I suppose there will be many changes. A new life to settle into."

"Yes." Jacob swallowed. How could she seem so nonchalant about that fact?

"You know, it could make the transition easier if we were to continue this marriage. If we adjusted to this new life together."

Jacob's breath hitched. As much as he wanted to agree, was it the best idea? If they continued the ruse, there would be no going back. Once they were seen sharing a roof, their marriage would be considered consummated, whether it was or not. Had

Dawn considered all this? Or did she simply crave the comfort his presence provided?

"Dawn," he began.

"I am sorry. I should not have suggested..."

Jacob stopped and put a hand on her arm. He peered into the face that he would not mind looking upon every day for the rest of his life. "Dawn, I am more than willing to stay married to you. But are you ready for that? For forever?"

Dawn swallowed. "Are you?"

He raised his brows, and the corners of his mouth threatened to pull upward. "I asked you first."

"I just do not want to make a mistake."

Jacob leaned back from her, as though he had been struck. "Would being married to me be a mistake?"

"Never," Dawn replied immediately. "But you might come to believe it was a mistake to marry me."

"Dawn! I would never think it was a mistake to be married to you. Why would you think that?"

She blinked, tears shining in her eyes. "Because of my... my..." She glanced down.

Jacob sucked in a breath. "Because of your hand? How could you ever think that would become an issue? It has never been a problem." What else did he have to do to make her believe?

"I know. But what about..." Her mouth worked, and she looked to the side. What was on her mind? "Later...when there are children. Or when I need help."

Jacob took her hand and her stump into his hands. "Dawn, I could never..."

"Me need to pee." Mary's little voice stopped him in his tracks.

Dawn slipped from his grasp. "Of course, dear. Slide on down here." Mary slid right into Dawn's waiting embrace, with no difficulty at all. How could a woman as capable as she ever see herself as a burden? He might never know. And now, he might have lost his chance to find out.

~

"Oh, look at that," Dawn exclaimed, gazing heavenward. Jacob angled his head in the same direction, but all he saw was the green upon green of the canopy of leaves.

"Paw paws." Dawn pointed to a large green object hanging on the tree. Actually, once he focused, there were dozens of the large, oddly shaped balls.

"What is a paw paw?"

"A fruit."

Jacob glanced between Dawn and the strange-looking object she claimed was a fruit. It did not appear appetizing in the least. "Do you want one?"

She sighed and looked around. "If there was one hanging low enough."

Jacob chuckled. Perhaps this was his moment. 'Twas not exactly how he had imagined winning her heart, but he had learned long ago that life with Dawn was always a pleasant surprise. And after their conversation earlier, he had hope that he might already hold her heart, that it was only reassurance that she needed. "Oh, my dear Dawn. I have brothers. You do not believe I know how to climb a tree?"

Her eyes widened. "Climb the tree?"

"Yes. I did so in the war, too, sometimes. Samson knows how to stand ground tied behind a bush while I climb a tree. In case we needed to hide."

Dawn gave a small giggle.

"Just watch and see." He winked.

Jacob quickly regretted the decision, for the tree was much harder to climb than he remembered, the rough bark biting into his hands. But if he could impress the woman waiting at the bottom, perhaps it would all be worth it. He finagled his way out onto a branch and shimmied down to where it began to bend under his weight.

"Jacob?"

"Do not worry," he assured her, though he had no inkling of how he would reach the paw paws that were still down at the ends of the branches. He straddled the limb and looked around to see if there was one on an upper branch he could reach. There. Carefully, he came to a kneeling, perched on the branch. He stretched toward the elusive green fruit, but it was still out of reach. He stretched a little farther. Just a bit more.

The branch beneath him gave as he shifted, dropping lower and throwing off his center of balance. Jacob's eyes widened a moment before he felt the pull of gravity. He clamored for the branch as he passed but barely managed to scrape it with his fingertips.

All too soon, he landed in a heap on the ground, his left ankle crunching beneath him. "Ahhh," he hissed.

"Jacob," Dawn screamed and rushed toward him. She was by his side and examining him before he could even process if his ankle was his only injury. "What hurts?"

"Uh, just my ankle." No, his hands throbbed as well. And his pride was hurt worst of all.

～

To Dawn's panicked assessment, Jacob's only serious injury appeared to be his ankle, his foot bent at an odd angle beneath his other leg. He rose enough to pull the joint out and stretch the limb straight. He tried to hold in his sound of pain, but she did not miss the sharp intake of breath. This was not good.

Dawn ran her hand down the leather of his boot, then

looked to his pained face. "I will need to remove this boot to fully examine it."

Jacob nodded.

As gingerly as she could, Dawn pulled the boot free. Thankfully, the foot did not flop over once the support of the shoe was removed. The ankle was such a complex joint, though. Could he have a break down inside the joint or the foot? Carefully, she prodded around. She flexed the foot forward and back, ignoring the fact that she had never embraced him in such a way, never felt the strength of his muscles. Jacob remained stoic through it all, making her assessment all the more difficult.

The way his mouth was still pressed in a line showed he was still in pain, but there was question in his eyes. Perhaps he was not too injured, after all. "I cannot feel anything broken," she said. "What do you think?"

"As bad as it hurts, I believe it is just sprained. You know I do not want to do this to you and Mary, but I believe I will need to ride Samson to continue on." Despite his obvious injury, he raised his brows, wordlessly asking permission to ride while she walked.

In many ways, Jacob continued to prove he was different from others, that he actually considered her feelings. She wanted to believe it with all her heart—that they could have a future. But the same question lingered in the back of her thoughts. Would he see her as a burden on down the road?

"Jacob, I would not have it any other way. We cannot have you injuring yourself further."

Jacob reached down and pulled his boot back onto his foot, breathing out as he did so. His body was mere inches from hers. A familiar scent wafted around her. She could not place the source—a soap or something, perhaps. But she closed her eyes and inhaled. And suddenly, she was there on the bank of the pond with Jacob sitting so close that their fingers were practically touching, laughing about some joke he had told her.

Back then, she had not considered the future or whether he would change his mind. All she had known was that he was the best friend she had ever had besides her father. And she had simply allowed her desire to be in his presence to guide her.

A hand touched her face, and a tiny gasp escaped at the sensation of skin against skin. Her eyes popped open to reveal Jacob's brown eyes, his brows lowered in concern. No matter how his face had changed, those eyes had not changed. "Dawn, are you well?"

She nodded, but no words came to her. Both his closeness and that familiar smell that transported her back in time were too distracting. Why could she not lean into this? Lean into the comfort she found in his presence? Lean into the way he accepted her better than anyone?

"Jacob," she finally whispered, but she had no other words to follow that one.

"Yes." His voice was husky, barely more than a whisper either. And she could feel his breath on her skin. On her lips.

Jacob was so close. Could she let him in? Could she trust that God brought them back together?

In the next moment, the gap between them closed. She knew not if she had bridged the gap or he had, but it did not matter, for his lips pressed to hers in the sweetest union she could have ever imagined. The kiss held all the qualities Jacob did—sweet and accepting, attractive and teasing. It made her want to press further into the kiss. So she did. Jacob brought a hand up to her shoulder and matched her response.

Could being married to her best friend truly be this sweet? Dawn pulled back and swallowed. There was no threat before her, though, no look of disapproval or disdain. Only Jacob's familiar face with a look of tenderness and possibly...love?

A blur rushed toward her from the right, and she whipped toward the movement. A small body slammed into theirs, embracing both her and Jacob around the neck. Mary did not utter a word, but Dawn found herself wrapped in a hug with both Jacob and the child.

What about the kiss had caused Mary to react in such a way?

"What is wrong?" she asked when the child sat back on her heels.

Mary shook her head and grinned. "Me happy."

Dawn tilted her head but reached out and squeezed her little hand. "I am glad." Whatever brought the child joy, brought her own joy. But she was still perplexed by the child's response to their kiss. At least she did not resent their closeness, though. That was another hurdle passed.

Perhaps it was best for them to have their midday respite now and give Jacob's ankle time to rest before they journeyed on. "We will unload some of Samson's burden before we continue on, but we should go ahead and take our respite now and eat the bread and cheese."

Jacob nodded. "That is a good plan. But when we reach the station, we switch places." He leveled a pointed look at her, but the corner of his mouth was lifted.

Oh, how sweet and stubborn. "We will see," she conceded with a grin of her own.

Somehow, they were able to enjoy their meal without any awkwardness. And true to his word, when they were within sight of the station, Jacob reined Samson in.

"Time to switch," he said.

They stood at the edge of the tree line, with the station at the top of the hill. The vast log wall forming the front of the fortified settlement stretched wide on that horizon, beckoning them forth.

Dawn inclined her head toward Jacob's ankle. "Are you sure you need to be walking on it?"

Jacob slipped to the ground but did not allow the injured

leg to catch his weight. Then he attempted to mask his limp as he turned toward her. "I will be fine."

Dawn crossed her arms and raised her brows.

Jacob only grinned. "Come on. Up my ladies go." He nodded toward the saddle.

"We will load our packs back onto Samson, but we should all walk to the station. Together."

Jacob watched her for a second. "All right."

Once that task was complete, Jacob, with the reins in his right hand, extended his left toward her. Dawn clasped onto it and all the strength and confidence it held. Then she turned to Mary but frowned when she remembered that she could not take the child's hand from that side. How could she ever hope for a family with her condition?

But, to her surprise, the little one did not bat an eye. Instead, much as Jacob had done on occasion, she grinned her bright grin and wrapped her little hand around Dawn's wrist. Then she turned toward the station, head held high.

Tears pricked at the backs of Dawn's eyes. These two loved her and accepted her exactly as she was, deformity and all. To them, it made no difference. She could barely consider a time when her heart had pressed with such joy.

CHAPTER 12

Her husband is known in the gates, when he
sitteth among the elders of the land.

— PROVERBS 31:23

July 4, 1782
Bryan's Station, Kentucky

Jacob gritted his teeth as he did his best not to limp, but pain shot through his ankle and radiated up through his leg with every step. Dawn needed him to be strong, though, and he could not allow the first impression he made at the station to be that of a weak, incapable man. As they neared the structure, a shout could be heard from above. Then the tall wooden station gate swung just wide enough for them to enter.

As soon as they were through, a man shut the gate and pulled the bar down. What was called a station by name was actually a fort with palisades and turrets at each corner. The structure was incredibly long, with what appeared to be around twenty houses built along the length of the two longer sides.

Several men approached. The hair on the back of Jacob's neck stood up, and he gripped Dawn's hand tighter. He managed to pull himself taller despite the pressure it placed on his ankle. He could endure the discomfort if only he focused on the problem at hand.

The first man to reach them held a rifle and wore a black hat and waistcoat. His eyes were almost as dark as the garments, and his jaw remained set until he opened his mouth to speak. "Welcome. Did you encounter any trouble?"

"No. We traveled from Richmond, and despite word of attacks, we encountered no threats along the way."

"Good." The man's gaze slipped to the gate, up to the lookouts, and then back to Jacob. "What brings you to our station during this time of unrest?"

Jacob nodded toward Mary. "This child here. She had received word that this was where her uncle was stationed. Both her parents have passed, and"—he glanced at Dawn—"while my wife and I would be more than glad to continue as her guardians, we felt it best to return her to family, if possible."

Dawn squeezed his hand.

The man gave a curt nod, then looked at Mary. He squinted as he assessed her, likely to try to determine if she bore a resemblance to anyone he knew. "What is her uncle's name?"

"Edmund. Edmund Fairfax."

"Oh. I did not realize he had any family. I will take you to him, though." He led them to a cabin near the front of the fort and knocked on the doorframe of the open door. "Edmund, it is Morgan."

A moment later, a man wearing a Continental Army uniform appeared in the doorway. He stood a few inches taller than Jacob, and his blond brows pulled together as he surveyed his guests.

Their guide provided explanation. "Edmund, these newcomers say you are this girl's uncle."

"Her father was Ethan." Out of the corner of his eye, Jacob caught the movement as Dawn rubbed her hand across the top of Mary's back, between her little shoulder blades.

"Ethan's girl?" Edmund's eyes widened as he turned to take in Mary. "Come. Come in." He stood to the side and held out an arm to invite them into his home.

"Here, I will tie your horse," the first man offered.

They followed Edmund into one of the single-room matching homes that lined the two longer sides of the fort. He motioned them to a small square table with two chairs. Dawn gathered Mary into her lap as she sat. Jacob hesitated, not wanting to leave the host standing, but Edmund pulled a chair over from the corner of the room. Jacob settled in across from Dawn as Edmund set his chair at the side of the table.

"So...my brother...I thought that not hearing from him through the years simply meant he had been unable to get word to me here in the wilderness."

"I am so sorry, sir. She passed away two years ago." Dawn's soft, gentle voice was the best one to break such news.

Edmund nodded, but he blinked, his face reddening even in the dimness of the cabin. "And this is..."

"Mary. His daughter. She is four now."

Mary peeked up from where she had her face buried in Dawn's chest.

The man sucked in a breath. "She looks so much like her father."

"We received the last letter you sent saying you were here. We prayed you would still be here when we arrived, for you are all the family she has left." Dawn's voice caught.

"And you have been caring for her?"

"Yes. I am her stepsister. And this is my husband." Her gaze connected with his over the table. Jacob gave her a gentle smile.

"I appreciate all you have done. I know Ethan would be grateful to know his daughter was cared for. Do you plan to stay on here?"

"Yes, for some time at least."

"Then we should find you some lodging." Edmund pushed from the table. "With all of the unrest, there have been several families that have left for safer locations. Actually, the cabin right down from here became available just this week."

Jacob opened his mouth, then closed it again. His gaze darted from Edmund, to Mary, and back again. Did the man not wish to connect with his niece? Perhaps he only aimed to see to their needs first.

After they stepped back out into the afternoon sun, Edmund led them to another of the small, matching homes, four down from his. He pushed open the door. The stagnant air inside the building, which had been closed up in the heat of summer, was stifling as Jacob accompanied him inside. Jacob pulled a chair from the table and used it to prop open the door while Dawn followed them in with Mary.

The one-room cabin contained a table and chairs, a bed that appeared to have a trundle beneath, a fireplace for cooking, and a vanity and hutch. Disappointment crawled into Jacob's stomach and settled there. The dark room was so small and uninviting. He was not sure how he meant to provide it, but he had hoped for a better home for his family—one they could be proud of.

"I know it is not much." Edmund seemed to read his mind. "But it bears all the essentials, and if you find yourself in need of anything, you need only to ask."

"We certainly appreciate it." Dawn offered a small smile. Edmund still had not mentioned taking Mary in. Was she beginning to regret the decision to come here?

Edmund nodded, then looked to Jacob. "I can show you to where Morgan tied your mount so you may get settled. I figure it will be best for Mary to stay tonight with you. With it being the first night in a new place, she may need some familiar faces to ease the transition. I can show you around and introduce you to some of the others tomorrow."

Jacob let out a breath before he grinned. "Thank you." Finally, the man had made his intentions clear. It seemed he was the kind of person who liked to get straight to the point, without extra words. Though it might make it more difficult for him to connect with Mary, it would not hinder his ability to care for her. And he was already taking her needs into consideration. At least, Jacob hoped that was all.

~

July 11, 1782

With the scent of baking biscuits filling the cabin, Dawn took a moment to step away from the hot fireplace and move into the open doorway where a breeze ruffled the edges of her hair. She glanced down the way, but no movement could be seen at Mr. Fairfax's cabin. There never could be. But that did not prevent her from checking every morning, as though she could peer through the cabin walls and see that Mary was well.

In all reality, the child seemed to be adjusting to their new surroundings better than Dawn. Mr. Fairfax was often scouting or hunting during the day and unable to keep Mary, so she was more than glad to continue spending her days with Dawn. He had also introduced them to Mrs. Abbott, a widow with four children, who'd taken Dawn under her wing and helped her adjust to life at the fort. While Mary quite enjoyed playing with the youngest of the children, and Dawn was thankful for their presence in her life, a sense of anticipation lingered. As though she was still waiting for something to happen. But what?

Dawn sighed and retreated back into the cabin and to the pan warming over the fire. When she added four strips of bacon, they began to sizzle and pop. She closed her eyes and breathed deeply while her stomach rumbled in anticipation of the delicious food.

"Smells wonderful." Jacob echoed her thoughts as his shadow filled the door.

Dawn turned and smiled at the sound of his voice. "How is Samson?"

Jacob shrugged. "He seems to be settling well. I only wish there was better grazing."

Dawn frowned as she used a fork to flip the sizzling strips of bacon. To keep them safe within the bounds of the fort, all of the horses were restricted to a single, over-grazed corral. Though she understood the need for protection, it seemed inhumane. Samson, after having brought them thus far, deserved fresh air and green pastures, neither of which could be found in the crowded fort.

Jacob came and knelt beside her, rubbing a hand over her back. "He is well," he assured her, before leaning in and pressing a kiss to her cheek.

Dawn grinned, her insides swirling. Every touch and kiss was still so new and wonderful.

"I am scouting with Edmund again today. What will you and Mary do?"

Dawn attempted to mask her disappointment, but her shoulders sagged without her consent. "Mrs. Abbott plans to teach me how to bake bread over the open fire." Her mouth pressed into a line as she removed the bacon skillet from the flame and moved the plate to a towel on the table. While it was satisfying to learn a new skill to help her provide for her family, it was bittersweet. It seemed that she spent as much time with Mrs. Abbott as she did her new husband. And despite the small, loving gestures Dawn and Jacob shared, it seemed they were both still holding back, not yet giving of themselves fully. "Try not to be out too long?" Dawn moved to Jacob and leaned into him, giving him a coy smile.

Jacob let out a hearty chuckle as he wrapped his arms around her. "You know I will not be too long."

Dawn laughed and nestled her head into his chest, grounding herself in the strong, steady heartbeat that echoed in her ear. *Thank You, God, for my husband. Please help me to be grateful for his presence in my life and for the many blessings You have provided for us here at Bryan's Station. But please help us find a way to bridge this gap between us.*

At length, she pulled herself from his embrace and retrieved the pan of biscuits from the fireplace. "Here. Have a bite to eat before you head out."

Dawn prepared a plate for Jacob and herself before she wrapped a biscuit and bacon in a piece of cloth and set it aside for Mary. She took a moment to eat with Jacob prior to his departure, then hurried through cleaning up the dishes. Finally, she was able to collect the food for Mary and head toward Mr. Fairfax's cabin. She hurriedly crunched across the dry summer grass between the two cabins. Then she knocked on the door.

When the door swung open, Mary's face broke into a giant grin. "Dawn!" She wrapped her arms around Dawn's legs. Her excitement at seeing Dawn never seemed to waver, no matter how often she came by.

"I am sure you have already eaten, but I brought you bacon and a biscuit. Ready to go to Mrs. Abbott's?"

Mary nodded and silently accepted the cloth with that sweet look of contentment she so often carried. The cloth fell open around her little hand, and she ate as they walked. Together, they made their way across the fort to the second building on the right. Outside, Sarah and Abraham, the two youngest, played marbles on the porch. The twins were a year older than Mary, and both bore the same raven-black hair and chocolate-brown eyes Mrs. Abbott said was inherited from their father.

A cacophony of noise drifted through the open door.

"Me play?"

"Of course, dear." Dawn accepted Mary's half-eaten food and dropped a kiss on top of her head. Then she chuckled as Mary scampered around behind Abraham and knelt down, eye level with the glass marbles. Dawn lingered for a moment to watch the joy on her face before she stepped up onto the porch and knocked on the doorframe.

"Come on in, honey," Mrs. Abbott called.

When Dawn walked into the cabin, she was met by a flurry of activity. "Stand still, or I am going to stick you with the pin," Rachel, the eldest, admonished Ruth, who stood in a chair with a new blouse pieced together across her top. The eleven-year old who carried her mother's sandy-brown hair and hazel eyes seemed to suddenly tame the ants in her pants.

"Come, come." Mrs. Abbott motioned Dawn past the two girls to where she stood at the table beside the fireplace. "Perfect timing. This one is ready to go in. I need you to move a scoop of coals over to the hearth there." She pointed.

Dawn went to the hearth and picked up the metal scoop. Digging into the bright orange coals, she scooped up a portion of them and moved them over to a clear section on the stone hearth. "Next, we set this on top." Mrs. Abbott carried the baking kettle over to the hearth and settled it on top of the coals. "The legs will keep it from burning, and now, we need another scoop of coals on top of the lid."

Mrs. Abbot never seemed to think twice about Dawn's deformity, assuming she could complete any task she handed to her. And for that, Dawn was grateful. She scooped another portion of the hot coals and carefully scattered them atop the lid. "Perfect." Mrs. Abbott beamed. "And last but not least, add a scoop of ashes on top."

The woman did not wait and watch for the task to be completed, but simply moved on to the next item that needed her attention. Dawn added the scoop of ashes on top while the matron saw that the construction of the blouse was being handled appropriately by her eldest daughter. "Good. Good work," she praised the fourteen-year-old as she looked it over. Rachel released a small smile, her own chocolate-brown eyes warming as she continued working, her black hair curled into a neat bun at the back of her head.

"Now, Dawn, let us prepare the next loaf while that one is baking." She moved back over to the table. "You did bring Mary with you?"

"Yes. She is out playing with Sarah and Abraham."

"Wonderful." Mrs. Abbott stopped and gave her a genuine grin, the skin around her eyes and lips crinkling as she did so. "I do so love to see the children getting on with one another so well."

"Me too." Dawn pushed a smile onto her face. Life did seem easier when she was working alongside Mrs. Abbot and Mary was happily playing. But without her marriage having been consummated, she felt as though she was building a foundation on shifting sand. What was causing Jacob to hold back? Despite their declaration of a shared desire for a life together, she could not seem to bring herself to broach the subject.

And though Mary was still in their lives, it was not enough. No matter how Dawn pretended during the day, her heart was torn each and every time she had to leave Mary with Edmund.

CHAPTER 13

> Be strong and of a good courage, fear not, nor be afraid of them: for the LORD thy God, he it is that doth go with thee; he will not fail thee, nor forsake thee.
>
> — *DEUTERONOMY 31:6*

AUGUST 15, 1782

"I cannot wait to see Dawn's face when she lays eyes on these." Jacob lifted the stalks of flowers with bright red blooms all along their tops and grinned at Edmund. Guilt squeezed like a vice around his heart, though. Would any number of eye-catching flowers show his wife that he truly loved her, stump and all, if he did not consummate their marriage?

Edmund shook his head but smiled. "You are the only man I have ever seen to go out hunting and bring back flowers along with his deer."

Jacob chuckled. "The meat is a blessing, indeed, but I

thought of Dawn as soon as I saw these beauties. Nothing she loves more than nature." And now, after gaining her freedom, his poor wife was relegated to the bounds of the fort except for when the women fetched water from the spring. All because she was trying to do what was best for Mary. Meanwhile, breaking her own heart in the process.

Jacob frowned. Hopefully, these brilliant blooms would work to brighten both her spirits and their dim, dull cabin, despite how he withheld the one thing that would make their union true in every sense of the word. But how could he press her for that when Mary had been taken from her? When her freedom had been taken from her?

"Jacob?"

He turned toward Edmund and the question in his voice. "Yes?"

Edmund moved his horse closer as they plodded along toward the rear of the fort and nodded into the trees. Jacob's brow knit together as he followed his gaze. But then he saw it. The edge of a horse's nose. The flick of a black tail. Not one rider, but many, attempting to conceal themselves in the trees. He met Edmund's gaze and nodded to let the older gentleman know that he had seen the same danger as he.

Silently, they rode on. If their visitors had not revealed themselves yet, perhaps it was best to pretend that they had gone unseen. Still, apprehension crawled across Jacob's shoulder blades and prickled up the back of his neck as they reached the corner of the fort and rode down along its side.

Even though he kept his face pointed ahead, Jacob continuously swept his gaze over the forest. He sucked in a breath when he noticed the form of a barefoot, deeply tanned man perched in the top of a tree, only his lower half visible from behind the leaves. He did not appear to hold any weapon at the ready, though, for one hand rested on the branch beside his foot, and the other was on the tree trunk beside his hip. Still, it seemed both British and Indian forces laid in wait. Though the war was supposed to be over, there were British militia that joined with Indian tribes in the area in an attempt to gain control over the Ohio River Valley.

Jacob tempered his breathing and consciously loosened his grip on the reins. Samson would easily pick up on his apprehension and begin prancing if he were not careful.

As it was, the horse's hooves seemed to be slogging through molasses as the front of the fort drew closer at a disturbingly sluggish rate.

Finally, they reached and rounded the corner. Jacob and Edmund exchanged another glance. Were the inhabitants of the fort aware of the danger? Would they open the gates for them?

Almost as soon as the question had come into his mind, the wide gates cracked open. It did not ease the tension in his shoulders, for as long as the gates were open, the entire fort was at risk. Was this what their visitors were waiting for? He opened his mouth to ask Edmund if they should call ahead and have them close the gates. Instead, Edmund's black horse passed his at an extended trot. Jacob urged Samson to do the same, and the horse willingly complied, picking up the bumpy gait to quickly take them inside the opened gates.

"Close the gates! Close the gates!" Edmund yelled the instruction as he spun his horse in a circle once they had entered. Samson loped the final few paces as the gates were quickly closed behind them. Jacob and Edmund slid from their mounts and glanced around, but there were no arrows, battle cries, or bullets.

With his deer still laid over his saddle, Edmund led his horse over to the men who were working the gates. "We are surrounded. Do not let anyone in if you do not know who they are."

"Surrounded?" The man's eyes widened, but Edmund did

not wait around to supply additional information. He headed straight for the corner turret where the station master, Elijah Craig, lived. The door opened before he arrived. A young boy came out to take the horses from them so they could enter immediately. Elijah must have heard the raucous.

Jacob glanced around, then placed his bouquet of flowers on the ground beside the door. He followed Edmund into the dim cabin.

As Elijah entered the room, Edmund pulled himself tall and gripped his hands behind his back, all business. "We must prepare for imminent attack. The fort is surrounded."

"Indians?" Elijah stopped in his tracks.

Jacob gave a nod from where he stood next to Edmund.

"How many?"

Edmund exchanged a look with Jacob. "Difficult to tell."

"And they let you pass?" Elijah leaned forward and put his hands on the table before him. "What are they waiting for?"

Jacob shook his head. "I know not. The cover of night, perhaps?"

Elijah's frown deepened. "Alert everyone. I will send for reinforcements."

Jacob and Edmund both dipped their chins to signal their understanding before they turned from the table. "Dawn should keep Mary tonight," Edmund advised as they stepped back out into the afternoon sun.

"I agree." Jacob dipped his chin.

Without another word, Edmund strode off to warn families. It was strange, though—in the safety of the fort with the August sun spilling sunlight over everything, it appeared as though there were no threat at all. If only that were true.

With Samson and the deer taken care of, Jacob retrieved his flowers for Dawn and headed toward their cabin. He needed to speak with her first and foremost.

When he arrived, the smell of venison cooking over the fire

drifted out the open door, as well as Mary's soft giggle mixed with that of Dawn's. His chest constricted thinking of them in danger. No matter the obstacles that he and Dawn still needed to tackle, he loved her and Mary both dearly. If only the three of them could be a true family.

Jacob pushed a smile onto his face as he stepped up onto the porch and into the room. Dawn glanced up from where she tended to the meat in a pan over the fire. Her mouth dropped open at the sight of the flowers in his hand.

"Oh, Jacob, those are beautiful." She stood and came to him, Mary on her heels. Dawn took the flowers and lifted them to her nose, inhaling deeply.

Jacob scooped Mary up into his arms. "What are they?"

She gave him a demure smile. "Cardinal flowers. *Lobelia cardinalis*. Thank you." She pushed onto her toes and pressed a lingering kiss to his lips. Then she drifted across the room, petticoats swaying as she retrieved a cup of water to place the flowers in.

"You are welcome. But Dawn, there is something I must tell you."

Dawn turned, the smile falling from her face.

"There are Indians surrounding the fort. We must prepare for an imminent attack."

Dawn's eyes rounded, and she gripped the chair back beside her.

A knock sounded on the doorframe behind Jacob. He turned to find the same man in black from the day they arrived at the fort, Morgan.

"We have a problem."

Jacob's stomach dropped to the floor. What could be worse than being surrounded by enemy troops?

August 16, 1782

*D*awn glanced around at the familiar faces stricken with fear as they stood just inside the station gates. Most she recognized, but few of the people had ever spoken to her outside of when Mrs. Abbott had taken her around and made introductions when she first arrived. Though no one at Bryan's Station had ever outright scorned her, many still seemed reluctant to approach her. Even now, with the danger they were about to face, several shot glances her way, their eyes going to her missing hand before they turned back.

Dawn sighed and Mrs. Abbott squeezed her shoulder. She offered the woman a wan smile. Rachel and Ruth stood beside their mother, their eyes round and mouths crimped. Mrs. Abbott spoke up. "Ladies, I believe it is time to pray."

Dawn, Mrs. Abbott, and the girls knelt first. Then all the others followed suit. Though not part of their normal routine and at the risk of drawing attention from those waiting outside, a great cry for safety went up from their small crowd as the women begged God for a safe trip to the spring and back. Even when one woman finished praying, they each remaining kneeling until the last word of prayer had been uttered. Then they were able to stand with their chins held high, knowing that their God went with them and before them.

Dawn glanced back to where Jacob stood with his rifle a few feet away from the group of women, alongside Edmund and a couple of other husbands. All the color had left his face the night before when Morgan informed him they would run out of water if the women did not go to the well at the spring and fetch water as they did each morning. Jacob had gone with Morgan to speak with Elijah Craig, Daniel Boone, and the other men of leadership within the fort, and best she could tell, a serious discussion had taken place before it was determined that there was no way around it. The women had to go about their normal routine with as little change as possible. Dawn flashed a small smile in Jacob's direction—though it could do little to ease the worry he must feel—before she turned and joined the women filing out of the fort.

Some of the women carried their wooden buckets in hand, but a few others carried them on wooden beams over their shoulders as Dawn did. For Dawn, it was the only way she could fill more than one bucket. For others, it allowed them to fill four. And they would need every ounce of water they could carry should an attack come to fruition.

Even though they were not supposed to look about, Dawn could not keep her gaze from drifting into the trees. Nothing appeared out of place, but still her heart pounded in her chest. Was that a movement?

Dawn turned forward again, a shiver running down her spine.

'Twas best to distract herself by joining in on the conversations that a few of the women attempted to carry on. "Ruth, you have a birthday coming up soon, do you not?"

The girl giggled, then stopped and glanced about. "I will be twelve." She whispered, as though it was a secret.

Dawn chuckled. "Well, you will be a young lady, then."

"Ma says we can lower my skirts that very day." Ruth grinned proudly now, her fear forgotten in the joy of growing older.

Rebecca shook her head. "I keep telling her that it is not nearly as fun growing up as she thinks. All you do is work and no play." Though her voice held a teasing edge, she spoke the truth. As the oldest, a large responsibility fell upon her shoulders.

"Are we not working right now?" Ruth raised her brows and the buckets she carried in each hand.

"True," Rebecca agreed.

In truth, there were more girls than women present. And

yet, each one carried their own weight. It was the way of life on the frontier. And, in Dawn's experience, the way of life when you did not have parents of affluence who could provide for your care. In fact, Ruth and Rebecca's burdens were lighter than hers had been at their ages simply because of the fact that they were able to share the chores with one another. Family was genuinely such a blessing.

A woodpecker knocked on a tree overhead, drawing Dawn's attention. "Oh, but I believe this is a great adventure," she told Ruth, and for a moment, had even herself convinced. "There is always something new to be found, if only you look and listen. You see, that is the sound of a woodpecker. Have you ever seen one, hammering on a tree? I cannot tell what kind it is without seeing it, but most are black and white with a bit of red."

Rebecca chuckled. "I have seen one hammering on the house."

Meanwhile, Ruth's eyes widened. "There is more than one kind?"

Dawn nodded as the front of the group reached the well and began filling their buckets. "There are the downy and the hairy woodpecker. They look almost the exact same except that the hairy woodpecker is larger. There is the beautiful, red-bellied woodpecker. They have pale, almost white bellies, and the males have a lovely red crown over the tops of their heads."

"Only the males?" Rebecca turned back to the conversation.

"Yes. Unfortunately, in nature, it is more often the males that have the brilliant plumage or distinguishing features."

"That is not fair." Ruth plopped her hands on her hips, her buckets banging against her sides.

Dawn chuckled. Her efforts at distracting herself and the younger girls seemed to have worked, for they moved steadily closer to the well from which they would draw their spring water. "Cardinals are much the same. The bright red ones that you see are the males, and the females are mostly a drab brown that blends in with the trees. They only have a bit of red mixed in, and it is not nearly as bright."

"Still seems a shame," Ruth grumbled.

"Well, I suppose, for them, it is more important for the males to attract a mate and for the females to blend in and be more protected so they can tend to the babies."

Rebecca slid an appreciative glance at Mrs. Abbott, with a small smile tugging at her lips. "I suppose they would be lost should anything happen to their mothers."

Dawn had to blink back the tears that threatened at her eyes. "Yes. It is difficult to lose a mother."

Thankfully, it was their turn to draw water, so their conversation fell silent. Without any assistance, Dawn filled each bucket one-handed, then positioned her beam under them so she could lift it onto her shoulder. The task was not easy, by any means. But hauling water was not an easy task in general, especially for the younger girls. Still, soon every bucket was filled and they had begun the uphill climb back to the fort.

With the heavier loads and more difficult travel, little conversation could be heard over the panting breaths and the grunts that accompanied their labored steps. Their only focus now was returning safely. Would they continue to be spared, or would they be attacked now, when they were at their weakest?

Dawn had a knife in her pocket, but it would do nothing against arrows and bullets. That was, if she could even reach it in time to protect herself at all. Sweat slid down the side of her forehead, and she used her free arm to wipe it away, then blew out a breath.

The fort loomed just ahead.

The gates creaked open and the sliver of clearance between the two looked like hope. But would the enemy take this opportunity to move, while the gates were open? Her gaze darted to the tree line again. Still, no movement could be seen, and the women passed through the gates without incident.

Jacob rushed to Dawn and lifted the beam balancing the buckets on her shoulder before the gates even had time to close. When he wrapped his arms around her tightly, she melted into him, allowing her tears to fall.

How could this be the life that she had brought them to? With danger pressing in, the station walls seemed taller and closer than ever, so much of their freedom stripped away. Mary was no longer at risk of starvation, but now she was at risk of being killed in an attack. Traveling with Jacob, she had tasted freedom, tasted what it would be like to have a family. And now her heart yearned for it more than anything.

CHAPTER 14

> For we wrestle not against flesh and blood, but against principalities, against powers, against the rulers of the darkness of this world, against spiritual wickedness in high places.
>
> — EPHESIANS 6:12

"*I* will keep them safe," Mrs. Abbott assured him before she closed her door behind him a little later the day the women risked the trip to the spring. Jacob had full faith that the woman would do her best to ensure the safety of every single person under her roof, but it did little to ease the knot in his middle. If they were to come under attack, no one could guarantee their safety save for the good Lord above.

Jacob fell to his knee at the edge of the porch. *God, I know I have had little time for You for quite some time, but please do not hold that against me. Please forgive me of my transgressions and keep Dawn and Mary.* Jacob stood and took a deep breath before he started toward Elijah's cabin, where Edmund and several other men convened to discuss next steps.

Behind him, an eerie scream rent the air. Jacob turned on his heel to see tiny objects flying over the back wall of the fort. Arrows. They were under attack! "Get inside! Get inside," he screamed at the few people who had been milling about, but who now seemed to be frozen in fear. Then he took off running toward Elijah's.

As he neared, Morgan exited the home and ran past without acknowledging him. Still, Jacob went inside. "They are attacking the back wall!"

Edmund nodded. "Morgan has gone to determine the risk and report back."

The minutes seemed to tick by, one minute for every ten as they awaited the man's return. Elijah, Boone, Edmund, and several others all filled the small space, leaving no room for pacing. Jacob flicked his gaze from man to man, but no one spoke. Instead, an eerie silence fell over the station as her inhabitants took cover from the assailants. Only gunshots and an occasional shout came through the open doorway.

Finally, Morgan's build blocked the sunlight streaming in. "There is a small band of Indians attacking the back wall, causing more of a raucous than a threat. It cannot be all of their men. I believe it to be a ruse to draw us out."

Elijah frowned. "We will send out a small group to test the waters. See what their plan is."

"I will go," Jacob volunteered as he stepped forward and pulled himself taller. Perhaps this was his chance to finally prove himself capable in battle. And he could not imagine sitting around waiting for another moment longer.

Edmund shook his head. "You have a wife and..." He stopped and looked to Elijah. "I will take a handful of the single men with me. Just in case. There should be little threat to life, but I would not want to risk someone with a family simply to provide a distraction." He turned back to Jacob. "You and the others should stay here and provide defense should this draw the rest out."

Jacob's jaw clenched, but he did not protest. The man had a point, though if Edmund considered Mary his, then he, too, was a family man. Did he still not see the girl as his own? As it was, what happened if he were to be killed?

While a group of men readied themselves to venture outside the fort, the rest of them prepared to defend the structure from the inside. All along the walls were portholes that allowed for a rifle barrel to be pushed through. A man was stationed at every porthole as well as in the four turrets at the corners. Another group stood at the ready within the fort, ready to defend the gate.

Jacob found himself at a porthole near the back of the fort. Despite not knowing how the events would unfold, he sat preparing balls and patches. If he had that much ready to go, he would only need to measure his powder between shots. Hopefully, it would not be needed, but 'twas better to be prepared and not need it than to need it, and not be prepared.

Still, Jacob kept an eye on the front of the fort. The gates opened, and Edmund led the group of volunteers out on their horses. Immediately, shots volleyed. Edmund and his men swung their horses around, their mounts eating up what little ground they had covered. But then a couple new riders joined them. Two Indians came flying up through the ranks on their quick little speckled steeds. "No," Jacob screamed as they whooped and hollered their blood-curdling battle cries, torches in hand.

The men protecting the gate could not safely fire upon the Indians until they had passed their own men. Even after they did, they somehow continued on without taking a hit. Jacob stepped forward for a better vantage point, his eyes widening as the two riders split off in opposite directions and cast their torches onto the porches closest to them.

"Dawn!" Jacob abandoned his post and sprinted toward Mrs. Abbott's cabin where one of the torches landed, the orange flames already beginning to grow. "Fire! Fire!"

There were others much closer, but he yelled, anyway, in hopes that it would draw out Dawn and the others. Someone was there with a bucket of water before he even reached the porch. Then there was Mrs. Abbott with a blanket, beating the flames into submission. Still, his legs pumped.

By the time his boots hit the porch, the flames were out and his breaths came heavy.

"Jacob. Come in, darlin'." Mrs. Abbott motioned him into the house as she shook out her blackened blanket.

Finally, Jacob came to his senses. He glanced toward the entrance to ensure that all danger had passed. The gates were closed, and people milled about the now-deceased Indians and their horses. The men must have finally hit their mark. All seemed under control, so Jacob took the opportunity to go to his wife.

As soon as he set foot in the house, Dawn came to him and wrapped him in a hug. Mary ran up and latched her little body around his leg. "Everyone was so scared." Dawn pulled back enough to look up into his face, tears in her eyes.

How was it that they had been brought to this same situation with her in tears and clinging to him for comfort twice in a single day? And would it even be the last? For the day was not over yet.

"I know," Jacob whispered and tightened his embrace. He nestled his face into her neck while he held Mary close with his other hand. What would he have done if he had lost either of them?

Jacob clenched his teeth. He had to find some way to ensure their safety, whether it was removing them from the fort and the turmoil this land carried, or eradicating the threat. But even if this threat was eliminated, what about the next?

⁓

*T*his was all Dawn's fault. If it were not for her and her drive to reunite Mary with her uncle, they never would have been in this situation. But if she had never confronted her stepfather about going to Bryan's Station, she and Mary would still be under their stepparents' thumb. And that had been another kind of nightmare.

Perhaps she could have forgotten her goal once they were in Jacob's care, though? Then both he and they could be safe with his family in western Kentucky where the tensions were not so high.

Still, that was not the case either. There was no reason to regret what was in the past. Then she would not be married to this man who held her so tightly. If only they could bridge the one gap that still separated them.

Dawn took a deep breath and stepped back from Jacob.

"Everyone is well?" Jacob glanced from her to Mary, who had relinquished her grip on his leg.

Despite the scare she had suffered, Dawn nodded. "We are well." No matter how the day's events had worked to sever the threads of her nerves, she and Mary had come to no real harm. Everyone was safe, and that was all that mattered.

Suddenly, shots seemed to ring out from all around. Dawn jerked and ducked, then glanced about. Though the sounds were all around, there was no immediate threat.

Jacob squeezed her hand. "I have to go."

Dawn nodded, but her heart constricted as she watched him go.

Mrs. Abbott flapped her arms at those still in the cabin. "Come on, children. These men are going to need sustenance. Rebecca and Ruth, go to Mrs. Brooke and help her tend to any injured. Let us know if you run short on hands, though I pray you do not. The rest of us will prepare food and relay food and water to the men. They are not likely to stop to eat, but at some point, they will become hungry. It is our job to sustain them."

Mrs. Abbott's speech pulled everyone together. Any sense of fear and panic quickly transformed into a sense of purpose as every single one of them, from the youngest to the oldest, assumed their tasks.

Mary and Mrs. Abbott's two younger children stayed behind to help with the food while Dawn took a bucket of water and ladle, offering drinks to the men. A couple seemed parched already and grateful for a quick drink, whereas most declined so early in the battle. Next, Mrs. Abbott had prepared a basket of bread for Dawn to take around. Most of the men declined the bread as they readied their next shot, but a couple took a piece and shoved it in their mouth, nodding their thanks. Arrows flew over the walls and landed near Dawn and the men. Meanwhile, shots peppered the walls of the fort. Thankfully, few penetrated the thick wood put in place for such purposes.

At first, Dawn flinched at every shot, but the longer she was out, the more the shots simply became noise and she went about her business, watching the skies for arrows.

When she returned to Jacob, his eyes widened at the sight of her. Then he moved to her. "Dawn, you are back."

"I come bearing bread this time." She lifted the basket in her hand.

A shot ricocheted off the rim of the porthole. Dawn jerked. Jacob pushed her back toward the building behind them, farther from danger. "It is not only Indians, but British as well. So many of them. We will need sustenance, but we will need munition more. Tell Mrs. Abbott. She will know what to do or will know someone who will." He planted a quick kiss on her lips. "Be careful."

Then Jacob was back at his post, using the ramrod to load the ball and patch and pouring in a measure of powder. Dawn tore her eyes from him and darted back toward Mrs. Abbott's. She leapt onto the porch and dashed inside. "Jacob says the men need munitions more than anything. We are surrounded by British and Indians."

"Oh, dear." Mrs. Abbott spoke the words as if a small child had simply fallen and scraped their knee, not as though they were in the middle of a battle for their lives. "I should have known. Morgan runs the magazine room, but he may need assistance in assuring that each man has what he needs. Abraham, take a bucket and water around to the men. Mary and Sarah, stay here. I will be back soon. Come." She motioned to Dawn.

Dawn followed her from the cabin and to the magazine room she spoke of. The doors stood open to reveal a room filled with tables, crates, barrels, and weapons. The smell of black powder met Dawn's nose. Mrs. Abbott stepped over the threshold. "Morgan, do you need an extra pair of hands to relay supplies to the men?"

"Yes." Morgan motioned Dawn over without looking up from his task. Mrs. Abbott gave her arm a quick pat before she slipped from the room.

Dawn skirted around a table covered with rifles and moved over beside Morgan to find that he was preparing crates with balls, shot patches, and powder horns. He stopped, and his mouth crimped at the sight of her. His glance took her in from head to toe.

"Can you handle this?" Much to her surprise, his tone was not one of judgement. He only needed the truth.

"Yes." She nodded. "If you continue to load the crates, I can deliver them to the men. And I should be able to carry two at a time so long as they are stacked one on top of the other."

Morgan jerked his chin in understanding, then set back to work. They formed a relay with Morgan preparing the crates of supplies and setting them in stacks of two while Dawn delivered them to the men defending the fort. Once each man had received his first crate, she went through retrieving the empty crates for the process to repeat again. It seemed the supplies were being used faster than they could deliver them. Still, the day wore on and the fighting showed no hint of ending.

"Mrs. Dawn, do you need a drink?" Abraham came scurrying up behind her. His dark hair stuck out at all angles from sweat and exertion.

Dawn let a breath out as she lowered her empty crates to the ground and offered him a wan smile. These children were so resilient. She wiped the back of her sleeve across her own sweat-covered forehead before she accepted the ladle and drank of the thirst-quenching liquid.

"Come, Mr. Morgan will need a drink as well." Dawn motioned toward the magazine room with her stump before she bent to pick up the crates. 'Twas not as easy lifting them from the ground as from the tables, but she managed, even with her aching arms. Then she led Abraham over.

While the boy gave Morgan a ladleful of water, Dawn swept her gaze over the barrels that filled the relatively small room, many of which they had already emptied. "Morgan, is this all the supplies we have?"

He paused only long enough to glance her way, his mouth set into a thin line. "Yes."

Dawn swallowed. Would their supplies last, or would the fort be overtaken? What would happen then?

CHAPTER 15

> *But let judgment run down as waters, and righteousness as a mighty stream.*
>
> — AMOS 5:24

AUGUST 17, 1782

"We cannot simply let them go without doing anything!" A man named John spoke up from the crowd that had gathered near the front of the station. Although their assailants had tucked tail and ran in the middle of the night, men had begun to gather at Elijah's at first light to discuss what should happen next. Tensions were high and opinions divided, and the discussion had quickly poured out of the little cabin into the bright morning sunlight. Jacob stood next to Edmund to the right of the crowd with his arms crossed.

At the front, Daniel Boone raised his hands. Though he wore an unassuming brown waistcoat over his linen shirt and breaches, his sharp nose lent to his air of authority as well as his gray hair, earned through experience here in the Kentucky wilderness. "We are too far outnumbered. It would be unwise to follow them. I know William Bryan's loss was devastating, and that many of you want revenge for the destruction that occurred outside the fort walls and for the three men that were injured. But you would lose far more in a pursuit than you have as it is."

Every structure outside the fort had been burned to the ground while the siege was fought. While a few of the men such as Boone and Elijah Craig attempted to talk peace, men were outraged, including those who bore injuries. One man stood in the crowd, supporting the move to send a party after their attackers, despite his arm hanging in a sling after having sustained a shot.

"We could ambush them, attack them while they are on the run," another man yelled out.

"They are not on the run. They have retreated because they realized they could not penetrate our station walls. The element of surprise is not a given."

Jacob spoke up. "What if it could be?" He had to admit, sitting back and allowing the men who had attacked them to go free did not sit right with him either. When that bullet had ricocheted, Dawn's life had flashed before his eyes. And when he saw Mrs. Abbott's cabin on fire... How could he do nothing? "We could scout out their location, keep a safe distance away, and attack when they are least expecting it."

"As though they will not be sending scouts out as well? I cannot condone this." Elijah crossed his arms.

"I would certainly caution against it." Daniel Boone's face was grim.

"Well, I cannot sit idly by! Sometimes decisions should not be based on what is safe but what is right. Anyone that wants to fight, come with me!" Jacob knew not the name of the man who yelled out, but his face was nearly as red as the hair on his head, possibly more so. Shouts of agreement resounded.

Boone and Craig seemed to have lost control of the meeting as men marched off toward the magazine room. Morgan led the group, but would there even be enough ammunition left to adequately supply an attack party?

Jacob frowned and waited. Edmund remained at his side rather than heading after the others had Boone's and Craig's words of caution swayed him? If Jacob were a single man, he would not hesitate to follow the others, but he had not only himself to consider. Was it in Dawn's best interest for Jacob to stay back and defend them from the fort or to put his life in danger in an effort to eliminate the threat? He must do all in his power to ensure her and Mary's safety. "I will go." Edmund finally spoke up. "These men cannot go unpunished."

"I will go as well." Despite Elijah's earlier rebuttal, an experienced scout could still be needed on the trip.

Edmund frowned down at Jacob, his blond brows lowered over his blue eyes. "I am not sure that is wise."

Jacob stretched taller. "What do you mean?"

"It may be advisable for one of us to stay behind with Mary."

Jacob's fists clenched at his sides. "And it is better for you to go than I?"

"You have Dawn as well."

"Most all of the men going will be leaving wives behind." He flung his arm in the direction of the group moving toward the magazine room.

"They have no one else to go in their stead. You do."

Here he was all over again, being asked to stay behind with the women while everyone else pursued the noble fight. Suddenly, the choice was clear.

"If it is right for them, then it is right for me." Jacob lifted his chin and leveled his gaze at Edmund.

The older man's jaw worked before he dipped his head in a nod. Perhaps he had grown to feel protective over Jacob? After all, they had all become an odd family of sorts. Jacob had never held it against his father for trying to protect him either. But he could not allow his future to be dictated by someone else. Or to stand by and allow others to take action in his place.

Jacob followed Edmund to the magazine room where a large crowd had gathered. It seemed that the majority of the men, including the reinforcements Elijah had sent for, believed pursuit was the best course of action.

Morgan did his best to see to it that each man was equipped with two guns, whether they were their own or the fort's, as well as a substantial amount of shot supplies. Hang fires, when the trigger was pulled but the gun did not fire, were not uncommon with the black powder rifles that each man carried. During battle, one could not take the time to find what was wrong with the weapon. Instead, it was best to switch to another rifle if multiple hang fires happened consecutively. Thankfully, the only time Jacob had dealt with such was in training with the Continental Army. Additionally, he already carried both a rifle and a pistol, so he had no need of additional arms.

Still, as he assessed the crate of supplies Morgan had handed him, a fission of fear wound its way through his middle. Jacob tamped the sensation down. This battle he prepared for was like nothing he had faced before. But was that not what he had wanted?

~

"Bad men gone?"

"Yes, my dear." Thankfully, when they had awakened that morning, the air had been blessedly quiet, and Jacob had been lying beside Dawn. She had hoped that the enemy's retreat meant the end of the fighting, the end of the nightmare, but the quiet had been so easily shattered when the men of the fort had met to discuss the next course of action. Discussion had quickly turned to shouting.

At length, that had subsided, though it was unnerving not knowing what was decided, and Jacob had yet to return.

Still, Dawn had taken solace in Mary's presence and the simple rhythm of homemaking, putting her newly learned bread-making skills to use. It was an incredibly satisfying feeling, to do something for those in her care simply because she wanted to, not because she was made to do so.

When Dawn heard Jacob's boot steps on the porch, her heart lifted. She wiped her hands on her apron and turned to the door with a smile. But the face of the man who entered was grim, mouth set in a line, and he carried one of the very crates she had spent the prior day delivering to the men. Suddenly, it was as though she could be knocked over with the slightest of breezes.

Jacob walked over to where she stood, now gripping the edge of the table. "We are going after them."

"What?" Her voice sounded as though she was in a tunnel. She settled into the chair beside her.

Jacob glanced at Mary, then back at her. "Not Craig or Boone, but the majority of us."

"Why are Elijah and Daniel not accompanying you?"

"They do not believe we should go. The group that is going is more than a hundred strong, though."

"Why do they believe that you should not go?" Why did it not reassure her to know they would be in such numbers? That did not seem to negate the danger.

"They believe that it is too dangerous." His jaw worked, and his glance flicked to Mary again.

Dawn stood and took his arm, steering him outside, onto the porch. "Why is it too dangerous?" Somewhere along the line, her fear had transitioned into anger.

Jacob seemed to deflate a little. "Because we will still be

outnumbered. They believe we will sustain losses. Possibly many."

"Then why are you going? If we are safe here, why are you going in pursuit of a fight?" Dawn searched the face of the man she loved, with his familiar brown eyes, but found no answers.

"Because they attacked us. They attacked the people I love. Either of you could have been killed." He threw his hands in the air.

"So you are going to go and get yourself killed instead?" Dawn regretted the words as soon as they had left her mouth. Most likely, Mary could still hear every word they said.

Jacob's jaw set. "Edmund is going too."

Dawn sucked in a breath. "You are both leaving us? What will Mary do if something happens to both of you?" Tears rimmed her eyes.

Jacob avoided her gaze. "I...I will not let that happen."

"You cannot guarantee something like that. You cannot." Her voice cracked. "What will I do if I lose you?"

Jacob took her hand and squeezed it. "I will do my best to come back to you. But they may need a scout. And I cannot just sit by and do nothing."

"You would not be doing nothing. You would be taking care of your family."

"I will be taking care of my family. Just not in the way you believe I should. We did what was right when we fought in the War of Independence, and I have to do what is right now. No matter the risk."

Dawn's face heated. There was nothing she could do to sway her husband. He was leaving her, after all, and far sooner than she had ever imagined. Their marriage was not consummated and might never be. That thought hit her like a punch to the stomach.

And Mary's uncle was leaving her too. The girl's only flesh and blood. Of course, he had not been around much since her arrival. Instead, she had still spent much of her time in Dawn's care. But what was she and Mary to do if neither of them returned?

Dawn turned and headed back into the house. Inside, she shoved her hands into the dough and began to knead it once more. It did not matter that she was overworking the dough and the bread likely would not turn out. She needed a way to harness the frustration and pain that bubbled inside. And her husband would not be here to impress with the loaf, anyway.

Jacob silently entered and started to pack. With a sigh, Dawn abandoned the dough and prepared him a pack of food to take. Her heart ached with every morsel that she added, every morsel that he may or may not live to eat, but at least he would not die of starvation.

Finally, Jacob stood at the door, laden down with supplies, with his pistol strapped to his leg and his rifle over his shoulder. "Goodbye, Dawn." He spoke softly.

"No go!" Mary squealed and ran toward him, attaching herself to his leg. Jacob knelt and hugged her little body.

Dawn fought the tears that pricked at the backs of her eyes as she went to retrieve the child. "He will be back, my dear." She barely managed to whisper the words as Jacob handed her over. Then her voice broke, and she buried her face in Mary's soft hair. She wanted to turn, to cling to Jacob and beg him not to go, but comforting Mary had to come first. Jacob's hand came to rest on her back.

Dawn knew not how long they knelt there beside the open doorway, with Mary wrapped in her embrace and Jacob's hand at her back. But then he was gone. And she could not stop the tears from flowing.

CHAPTER 16

Thou shalt not be afraid for the terror by night; not for the arrow that flight by day;

— PSALM 91:5

August 18, 1782

Jacob flipped the crusty slice of bread over in his hands again but still had not the slightest desire to take a bite. Dawn had graciously taken the time to pack it, despite the hurt and anger he had inflicted, yet he could not bring himself to eat it. Instead, Jacob's stomach coiled and knotted with each step Samson took, detesting any thought of food.

He sighed and turned his attention ahead, where two rows of horses and riders riding side by side stretched as far as the eye could see. Little could be heard over the creak of leather and the multitude of horse hooves trampling the earth. More than one hundred men strong, and yet hardly anyone spoke a word. An ominous cloud of silence engulfed their entire group, even the battled-hardened mounted Kentucky militia. While most of these men were soldiers or were frontiersmen quick to leap into action, it seemed the seriousness of the situation had truly registered with each and every one of them. And, of course, all were aware of how dangerous it would be to give their position away by carousing and carrying on.

Never before had the silence bothered Jacob as it did now. Growing up with four siblings, he had always welcomed any opportunity to experience a break from the noise. That, in a minor way, had added to the appeal of his time spent with Dawn all those years ago. For she was pensive and observant, not quick to ramble on or speak for the sake of speaking. It had not been uncommon for them to spend extended periods of time walking in silence or simply sitting in one another's company.

Now the silence crawled under Jacob's skin and made the back of his neck itch. He pulled at his stock, attempting to adjust it to where the late-summer heat was not so unbearable. But his breaths came no easier as the sweat rolled down his back.

What had propelled him to choose to come on this wild goose chase? Was it truly so important to make the ones that attacked the station pay for their actions? Would they even be able to, or would they themselves be picked off one by one in battle? Perhaps he should have thought his decision through longer, rather than allowing his stubborn pride to win out. Jacob sighed and forced himself to take a bite of the bread.

There was far too much at stake to make such rash decisions. And yet he had. Were it only his life on the line, he would not care to die for what was right. But his life was not his own anymore. He had Dawn and Mary to care for. Especially if Edmund were to perish. How could he have allowed them both to walk into the same hornet's nest? Dawn was right. What would she and Mary do should they both die?

God, please do not let that happen. Please protect Edmund, myself, or the both of us. No matter what, please, just let there be someone to take care of Dawn and Mary.

Edmund reined his black steed over closer to Samson. "I need to ask a favor of you." His tone was quiet but serious.

Jacob took in Mary's uncle in his blue and red of the Continental Army, his black three-cornered hat doing little to shade his blue eyes, which squinted against the sun. Since their arrival, he had come to deeply respect the man who had taken him under his wing. "Of course."

"I want you to take Mary."

Jacob frowned. It appeared he was not the only one whose mind was preparing for the worst. "You know I will see to it that she is taken care of if something were to happen."

"I do not mean only in the event that I perish. I want you to take her no matter what. Even if we both make it back. She is a darling child who has brought much light to my life in the little time I have managed to spend with her. But my life does not allow me to care for her as I should, and she would be much happier with you and Dawn. I...I do not want to see you travel down the road I have...forsaking family for fighting." Edmund's jaw worked. "I should have told you that before you made your decision."

Jacob took a deep breath, and a weight lifted from his chest. Nothing would make Dawn happier than if the three of them were a family. She had done all she could to provide what she considered to be best for the child, but no one could love Mary as Dawn did. They shared a special bond that could never be broken. And here, now, with there being a chance that he would never see them again, he wanted nothing more either. To see them again. To be a family with them. In every sense of the word. "Are you sure?"

"I am. I do not ask only because of our current situation. It has been on my mind for some time."

Jacob nodded. "Then, yes, gladly."

"Good. That is where she truly belongs." A weight seemed to lift from Edmund as well, for his face relaxed and he sat a little taller. Was it because his affairs were now in order or because the decision had been weighing on him so? Perhaps both.

Finally, Jacob was comfortable enough to finish the bread in his hand. But to consider Dawn and the effort she put into the meal made his chest ache again. He only needed to make it through this fight ahead, though, and he could set everything to rights.

'Twas not that simple, for an uneven battle loomed ahead of him. Yet now more than ever, he had something to hold onto. Hope loomed before him. Many men, including some in this company, had seen battle and returned to their families. His own brothers as well.

While the circumstances may not be in his favor, there was One who always would be—the good Lord above. Jacob had not read his Bible as he should in recent years, but in his youth, his mother had always shared verses with them each night. One of her favorites came to mind now. He whispered it quietly to himself. "'Fear thou not; for I am with thee: be not dismayed; for I am thy God: I will strengthen thee; yea, I will help thee; yea, I will uphold thee with the right hand of my righteousness.'"

God, please carry me through the battle ahead and keep me safe. Though bullets and arrows may fly, please direct them from my path and let me come to no harm. Please bless me with the opportunity to see Dawn and Mary once more and to make a life with them.

Jacob straightened in the saddle. While a giant army waited for him, he would not fear, for God was with him.

*D*awn scrubbed Mary's dirt-stained dress against the washboard just outside the Abbotts' cabin. Beside her, Mrs. Abbott and Rebecca washed laundry of their own. A hot, dry wind tugged at the loose strands of their hair while they labored over the washbasins full of hot water. Meanwhile, Mary played with Sarah and Abraham, rolling a large wooden ring across the grass only to go in chase of it. Dawn scoured the dress until it seemed the dirt had fled from the garment.

Only then did she allow herself a break to glance at the massive gate that closed them off from the rest of the world. Certainly, it would not reopen so soon after the group departed. But how long would it be before it did? How long should she wait before she could begin to expect them back? How long until she should be worried?

She should not be worried at all. No, she should be livid. Livid at Jacob for leaving them.

Dawn finished with Mary's dress and retrieved one of the petticoats which carried a layer of dirt and grime along the bottom and started scrubbing again. Tears pricked her eyes.

When a hand settled on her arm, Dawn jerked. She turned toward Mrs. Abbott's friendly face, softened with sympathy. "I know it is difficult, but 'tis best to keep busy and not think about it."

"What if he does not come back?" Dawn had not voiced her concern to any other person, and it was a relief to release the words rather than to let them roll around in her mind over and over. After all, Mrs. Abbott had experience in the matter and would know firsthand how to handle the grief should Dawn have to face it.

"Look at that little girl over there." Mrs. Abbott inclined her head toward Mary.

Dawn's gaze settled on the giggling girl with a giant grin.

"*She* is your family."

Dawn shook her head with a frown. "You know she is not." Mrs. Abbott was privy to their entire story, even the truth about how her and Jacob's marriage had come to be.

Mrs. Abbott gave her that no-nonsense, motherly look that said she knew better. "Yes, she is. No one in this world loves that child more than you do. And she loves you as her mother. She knows you are the one that loves her and takes care of her. Edmund took her in because he is family and he was asked to. But he is only trying to carry out an obligation, to do what is right. And now, there is a good chance that if your young man does not come back, neither will he. You need to grab onto what is right in front of you and hold onto it as tight as you can. And if you lose Jacob, that little girl will be what gets you through the loss."

Dawn braced herself against her washbasin, blinking back the tears flooding her eyes. Hearing someone else say that Jacob might not make it back was far more difficult than simply thinking the thought. Mrs. Abbott's words came from a place of experience and truth, though. Only two years prior, she lost her husband of twenty years. She had confided in Dawn that it was her love for her children that had seen her through. Likely, it was still what helped her on the rough days when the ache of the loss returned.

Dawn turned her attention again to where Mary played. The summer sun shone against her blond curls, turning them nearly white. It was true that Mary would always have her heart. No matter where they went or who entered or left their lives, her love for Mary would never lessen. She had been so tiny when she came into Dawn's life, requiring so much care and nurturing. Knowing the losses she had faced at such a young age, Dawn had been more than glad to fill the role of her caretaker. For two years, they had no one but themselves. And if it were come to it again, they would still have one another.

It would not mean that it would be easy, but it would make

it bearable. And she could bear any burden if she leaned upon the good Lord above and sought God's beauty in every day. She had no desire to return to dark days such as the ones she had faced before, but should that be her lot in life, she would face it as she had done before.

Dawn's shoulders sagged. Why had she ever tried to do anything besides embrace her relationship with Mary? To embrace the person that God had placed in her life in the capacity in which he had placed her? It seemed she had forgotten to be grateful for her grandest blessing. Dawn leaned forward against the washbasin as tears slipped down her cheeks.

Mrs. Abbott's hand came to her shoulder. "Honey, you were only ever doing what you thought was best for her. That is all we can do as parents. And sometimes, we learn from our mistakes and have to do better."

Dawn nodded and smiled through her tears. "I only pray that I have that same opportunity with Jacob."

Mrs. Abbott wrapped her in a hug. "I know, child. I know. I will be praying as well."

The kind gesture did nothing to abate Dawn's tears. They flowed unchecked as she squeezed the plump woman tightly, leaning into how motherly and wonderful the embrace was. After the loss of her parents, she never imagined she would find someone to care for her as Mrs. Abbott did in a maternal capacity. And there it was again—another incredible blessing that she nearly missed by wallowing in her fear and self-pity.

Dawn had never been one to allow those two sensations to dictate her life, so why would she do so now?

CHAPTER 17

> And I will execute great vengeance upon them with furious rebukes; and they shall know that I am the LORD, when I shall lay my vengeance upon them.
>
> — EZEKIEL 25:17

August 19, 1782

Jacob yawned and rolled his shoulders before he pushed his left foot into the stirrup and mounted Samson. All around, men swung up onto their mounts as well. Though the sun had barely risen, it was imperative for the militia to be up and traveling at first light in order to catch up with the enemy. Easily, the men formed two lines, and the horses resumed their tireless march. Edmund took up the position beside Jacob once more.

The morning was fresh and crisp, if a bit humid, and Jacob drummed his fingers against the wooden stock of his rifle.

Better to have the weapon at the ready, rather than in its holster on his saddle, should they fall under attack.

As they approached the Licking River, the horses traversed gentle rolling hills. Then they entered a flat expanse of open meadow land, filled with tall grasses and a few sparse wildflowers that reminded Jacob of Dawn.

Before they knew it, shouts could be heard from the front of the line. Colonel John Todd barked orders for those close enough to hear, and a relay rider came down alongside the ranks to shout the orders for the others. "Push ahead! Ford the river! Form ranks! Push ahead! Ford the river! Form ranks!"

Jacob's heart ticked up a notch. This was it.

The horses at the front of the line assumed a trot, and soon, Jacob was bouncing along on Samson as they drew nearer to the ford in the river. The wide, lower area in the water allowed the militia to easily cross over on their mounts. Most of the horses, Samson included, delved in without hesitation, water splashing up all around them.

Edmund's black steed shied sideways before being coaxed into the river. In the meantime, another rider found his way between the two of them. Jacob said a silent prayer for his comrade but kept his focus ahead as Samson pushed across.

Water poured from them as the horses trotted up onto the other shore. All the men held their rifles in hand now, not only to ready for battle as they formed ranks, but because any man worth his salt would have kept his gun above the water as they crossed. Now was not the time for hang fires or soggy weapons. Lives were at stake.

The militia formed three columns, Jacob falling into the left behind Lieutenant Colonel Daniel Boone. Despite his hesitations, the colonel had not allowed his men to enter into battle without him.

A moment later, they advanced.

Jacob swallowed and glanced around for Edmund, but he was nowhere to be found. Ahead of them loomed a long rise. What was Colonel Todd thinking, coming from the low ground like this? *God, please let him know what he is doing.*

Before Jacob and Samson had even crested over the rise, shots rang out. The rest of the line swung around and charged forward, Samson leaping into action as though he had been trained for battle. Jacob sat deeper in the saddle and gave short, steady tugs on the reins to settle him down. Once he had the animal at a smooth walk, he started loading his rifle.

When he had the ball loaded and the powder poured, he raised the weapon to his shoulder and brought Samson to a halt atop the rise. Jacob's eyes widened—for what must surely be two hundred British militia and their Indian allies stretched out as far as the eye could see. Their leader must have known the settlers were coming, and they rode right into the trap.

Jacob aimed to the right of Samson's thick, mane-covered neck, blew out the breath he had been holding, and fired a shot. It missed its target. He held the reins in his left hand to keep Samson at a slow, steady walk as he fell into a rhythm—ball and patch, ramrod, powder, aim, fire. All the while, he did his best to tune out the sound of gunshots from both armies as well as the thumps of the balls pelting the earth around him.

But when the first soldier fell at his hand, Jacob stopped and stared as the man sprawled on the ground. He had blond hair, much the same as Dawn or Edmund. The brown horse the man had ridden skittered aside and then took off, attempting to free itself from the danger.

Beside him, one of his comrades toppled from his horse, dead. Jacob loaded another shot, not hesitating to fire this time. Steadily, the line moved forward, pushing the enemy downhill.

All of a sudden, shouts and cries came from the other side. Indian braves had swung around the right end of the line, sandwiching Colonel Stephen Trigg's militia between the Indians and British.

In the next moment, it seemed, Colonel Trigg went down. Then, in the very next, Colonel Todd fell. "No," Jacob yelled as he watched their leaders crumple to the earth. Samson pranced in place, not knowing if he should move forward into the fray or back away from the danger.

The militia began to scatter. Horses and riders bolted, galloping back over the crest and down the hillside toward the river they had forded. Jacob hesitated, glancing toward the approaching enemy ranks before he turned Samson and followed suit. A couple of horses tripped on the uneven earth and fell, taking their riders down with them as they tumbled down the hill with horrific squeals. Jacob winced and lifted his reins, keeping Samson's head up and slowing him to a measured lope.

Behind them, a group of braves followed, firing arrows upon the men before they could make it across the river. In front of Jacob, an arrow sliced through a man's middle, and with the wooden shaft sticking from his back, his body slipped into the river. Jacob grabbed the reins of the horse and ponied it across with him to the other side.

On the riverbank, one man shouted a command and waved an arm as he turned back toward the enemy. A small group of men made a stand while the remainder, their numbers much fewer than before, finished crossing. Shots volleyed across the river.

Jacob turned back and finally sighted Edmund. He and his black steed were at the end of the line, protecting the retreating militia from their assailants. Jacob surged forward toward him, the extra horse still at his side.

An arrow pierced Edmund's middle. Samson continued forward, but for Jacob, time suspended. Edmund's hand went to the arrow, and he wavered. He urged his horse to step from the line, but the animal shied at a blast of gunpowder beside him. Edmund slipped and landed on the rock-strewn sand at the shore. His horse trampled his rider, then veered in their direction, the whites of his eyes visible in his panic. Jacob had no time to steer Samson away before the steed crashed into Samson's chest and then nearly took off Jacob's left leg as he plowed past. Samson squealed and reared, kicking at the air. Jacob's eyes widened as the sensation of falling tugged his body backward. He grappled for the saddle, but the reins ripped from his hand before he crashed to the hard earth.

"Ah!" Pain shot through his head, then there was nothing but black.

~

Laughter filled the cabin, warming Dawn's worry-wearied heart. Despite the stifling heat, delicious vegetables from the late-summer harvest filled their bellies, and the children were happy and healthy. For the first time since Jacob's departure two days prior, Dawn felt an odd sense of peace. With Mrs. Abbott and her children, she and Mary would never have to face another truly lonely day in their lives. Trials would come and go, but with the good Lord above and friends that cared deeply surrounding them, they could walk through the fire.

Oh how wrong she had been about family having to be of blood relation. Mrs. Abbott had taken Dawn under her wing and made her one of her own without the bat of an eye. These people, here, surrounding her as she dried the dishes Mrs. Abbott washed, were family by choice. A blessing she never could have dreamed on her own.

"'Tis a wonderful sound, is it not?"

Dawn glanced from the children and their game of marbles,

all crammed in the little space at the front of the cabin, to Mrs. Abbott. "Yes, it is."

"One day you will have more." The older woman nodded. "And though they will give you gray hairs, they will fill your heart a little more, each and every one of them. And you will thank God for their presence in your life, every day."

Dawn gave her a warm smile before they both turned back to the task of cleaning up the dishes from the evening meal.

Shouts drifted in through the open door, drawing everyone's attention. Abraham scrambled from the floor and dashed out onto the porch. Rebecca followed. A moment later, she poked her head back through the doorway, her eyes wide. "A rider just came in. I believe he has news of the battle."

Dawn exchanged a glance with Mrs. Abbott, though the woman's measured expression gave nothing away. As soon as she finished drying her hands on her apron, she put a hand on Dawn's arm. "Let us go and see." She barely dipped her chin, but the gesture bolstered Dawn's spirit. It was so soon, the rider might come bearing other news.

Together, they walked out into humid, late-afternoon air. The sun had already dipped behind the fort walls, and soon dusk would be upon them. At the front of the fort, though, a small crowd had already collected around the horse and rider. A woman in the gathering screamed and fell to the ground. Dawn stopped in her tracks.

"We do not know," Mrs. Abbott reminded her, putting a hand behind her back and gently propelling her forward. But it was as if Dawn had already been plunged into the depths of a frozen river. A chill wrapped around her, and her muscles grew stiff. Her gaze remained affixed to the young boy beside the horse, his hat crumpled in his hands as he delivered his news and answered questions. Elijah Craig was among the group, and he turned, running a hand over his face before he hung his head. This could not be good.

As they neared, the boy's blue eyes locked onto hers, then shifted to Mrs. Abbott. He visibly swallowed. No one spoke for a minute as more people gathered around behind, closing them in. Dawn watched and waited for the news that she knew would come. The news that would shatter her heart.

Finally, the boy's glance encompassed the group. "Colonel Todd's militia was defeated at the Licking River, with heavy losses. More than half the souls perished. Please prepare a place to care for the wounded, as they will start to arrive after sunrise." He repeated his message.

Dawn staggered backward a step and reached for Mrs. Abbott, who wrapped an arm around her and latched onto her elbows to keep her from falling. Instead, she slowly lowered her to the ground.

More than half. How many remained, then? What were the chances that Jacob or Edmund were among them?

Tears swam in Dawn's eyes, and a cry formed a strangled knot in her throat.

"Not here, my dear." Mrs. Abbott looked to someone above Dawn. "Rebecca, go to the cabin and watch the children. Bring Mary home after a half hour has passed."

Dry grass crunched as the girl walked away. Dawn's heart ached for Mary, who might have lost the only men to ever love her. A fresh wave of tears bubbled up and threatened to spill out. Dawn covered her mouth with her hand. Mrs. Abbott coaxed her from the ground and kept her wrapped in her supportive embrace as she led her to her cabin.

Once inside, she settled Dawn on the edge of the bed. Then she fetched a dishcloth, dipped it in the water in the washbasin, and wrung out the excess. Mrs. Abbott wiped the damp cloth over her face, refreshing Dawn's spirit slightly. At last, she could take a deep, fortifying breath.

Then the news washed over her again. More than half dead.

Her composure crumpled, and she planted her face in her hands.

The straw tick sank as Mrs. Abbott settled next to her and rubbed her back. "Cry what tears need to be shed, for you have taken a shock. But this is not yet the time to grieve, my dear. You do not know what tomorrow will bring. No one does except for God and the men who fought in the battle."

Dawn sniffed and nodded as tears leaked from her eyes and down her cheeks. But no logic could stop the sobs that shook her body, and Mrs. Abbott sat faithfully by her side, holding her as she cried.

In the three years since her mother had passed, no other person had held Dawn aside from Jacob. And now, it was likely she would never feel his strong embrace again. She cried into the woman's shoulder.

No matter how she had prepared herself and no matter the strength she had felt the day before, her spirit was shattered. Words and thoughts were wonderful until you were in the deep depths of the dark pit of despair. Then they seemed as futile as a broom in a windstorm.

Finally, after some time, her tears were spent.

Mrs. Abbott stood. She rewet the dishcloth and brought it to Dawn. "Come now, my dear. Mary will be home soon."

Dawn sucked in a deep breath and accepted the cloth. Dawn wiped down her face and neck. While the other woman wrung out the cloth and laid it over the edge of the washbasin, Dawn stood and ran her hand and stump over her clothing, smoothing it out. Then she reached up and did the same for her hair, attempting to tuck the loose strands back into their pins.

When the door opened, Dawn even mustered up a smile as Mary ran to her. "There you are, my dear." She wrapped her in a hug and focused on the feel of her little body in her arms.

Mary pulled back and looked at her with her wide eyes, her head tipped to the side. "What wrong?"

Dawn chuckled through the tears that misted her eyes. The child was so astute. "Nothing yet, my dear. Nothing yet." She wrapped Mary in her arms again as Mrs. Abbott and Rebecca slipped from the room. Together, they would face whatever came tomorrow.

CHAPTER 18

> That led them through the deep, as an horse in the wilderness, that they should not stumble?
>
> — ISAIAH 63:13

August 20, 1782

Jacob blinked, the edge of the Licking River and the carnage of the battle coming into view. His ears rang, and his body protested as he lifted his torso from the hard earth, but he was alive.

Thank You, God.

Edmund. The events before he blacked out came flooding back to him. He glanced around. There. Several yards away, where he had fallen from his horse and been trampled, lay Edmund's body. *Please, no.*

Jacob scrambled over on hands and knees, ignoring the pain that seared through his leather-burnt hands. When he reached Edmund's body, he flipped him over onto his back. But instead of wide, staring eyes, a pained grunt greeted him. His face split into a grin.

"You are alive!"

Edmund groaned again and nodded, his arm wrapped around his middle. "Barely," he breathed, his voice raspy. "I think my horse tried to finish the job that arrow started." Edmund coughed, and Jacob's eyes widened at the sight of crimson blood on his lips.

"Come on. We need to get you back to the fort."

"Ah, to Mrs. Brooke, our faithful nurse. She is a beautiful one." Edmund's eyes were closed now, but he only seemed to be focusing on breathing and not allowing the pain to take over his senses.

"Yes. And a widow." At least the man still had his humor. "I need to find us some mounts, then we will leave."

First, were they still in danger? He glanced up the hill, across the river. He should have thought to do so sooner, but his concern over Edmund had clouded his judgement. The enemy, as well as most of the survivors, must have retreated, for on the hillside across the waters, a handful of men worked to dig what likely would become a mass grave. Still, he would feel better once they were out of this open valley.

Jacob slowly worked himself to standing, where he wavered. His head pounded and his vision swam. Once he steadied, he looked behind them. To his amazement, there at the edge of the tree line, stood Samson. And beside him, the brown horse he had guided from the river. Jacob's mouth fell open. The good Lord above was certainly looking after them.

As he took a step, pain shot through his left ankle. He hissed out a breath, then continued, focusing on his destination rather than the pain. His body ached as well from his impact with the ground, but his stiffness seemed to ease a mite with movement. When he reached the horses and gathered up their reins, the leather bit into his hands. But nothing would stop him from returning to Edmund's side.

Once there, he knelt and placed a hand on the man's shoulder. "Edmund, are you still with me?" The man nodded, his mouth and eyes both pressed shut in agony. "I have to get you up on top of this horse." Another slow, measured nod.

Jacob positioned the chocolate-colored horse right next to them. Then he moved closer and worked his arms under Edmund's arms. Together, they managed to haul him upright, though Jacob supported most of the other man's weight. From there, Jacob used Edmund's legs as leverage to push him on up onto the saddle. Edmund loosed a long, loud groan as the arrow penetrated deeper into his body. But for the moment, the shaft seemed to staunch most of the bleeding. So despite the pain that would likely slice through the man with every step of his mount, it would have to stay put.

Jacob walked around to the other side and pulled himself up into his saddle with a grunt of his own. He tied the brown horse's reins onto his saddle, then took Samson's reins between his fingertips. Squeezing his legs, he urged the horse to walk on.

With the setting sun at their backs, and trusting that men digging the grave would check others for signs of life before placing them in the ground, they started toward the fort. Toward Dawn and Mary and a bright future together. Dusk would soon engulf them in darkness, but he trusted Samson and the good Lord above would see them through the night and they would come out the other side closer to home.

As they drew near the tree line, Jacob stopped and turned in the saddle. For a moment, he simply sat, taking in all the bodies scattered over the hillside and along the shores of the river. Every single one died fighting to protect this life of freedom they were so blessed to live. Always, he would remember their sacrifice. And never again would he take a single day for granted. Or a single moment spent with those he loved.

He gave Samson his head, allowing him to lead them on. Every sway of the horse's gait made his body ache and his head throb, but he imagined it was only an ounce of the pain that Edmund bore. Every so often, he glanced over at his comrade, but with the dark of night and the movement of the horses, it was difficult to tell if he still breathed.

Finally, hours after nightfall, Jacob halted the horses at a creek and slipped from the saddle. A groan from Edmund's direction let him know the man was still alive. Jacob moved between the horses while they drank and over to Edmund. He opened his canteen and lifted it to the man's face. "Here, take a drink of water if you can."

Edmund turned his head without opening his eyes and drank a couple of swallows of the liquid. Then he sagged back against the saddle. Jacob removed his waistcoat and laid it over Edmund's body. He took a swig of the water, then refilled the canteen. What a blessing that he always carried his canteen slung across his body. After, he climbed back into the saddle and turned them toward home again.

As the crickets singing in the night became his only company once more, he was transported back in time, to the day he and Joseph had joked about the crickets and the owls. How he missed his brother's smile.

For the first time since they had parted ways from his family, his chest ached with the pain of missing their company, their personalities, and most importantly, their love. With only the deep darkness looming ahead, the vibrancy of his family suddenly seemed the greatest blessing. One he had thrown away in his haste to prove himself.

Jacob scoffed. The only thing he had proven was proving to himself that family was more important than anything. Dawn and Mary meant more to him than anything in the world, more than any battle he could fight or accolade he could win. Nowhere he could go and nothing he could do would ever mean anything without them by his side. As soon as he made it to the fort and saw that Edmund was cared for, he never wanted to spend another moment away from his family.

With Edmund releasing Mary into their care, would that mean they were free to go where they wanted and live where they wanted? Could they seek out his land and rejoin his family? Jacob released a contented sigh. Though he was not sure what Dawn's stance would be on the matter, a new dream bloomed before him—to unite his new family with the one he grew up with. As Samson plowed forth into the darkness, Jacob resolved that he would speak with Dawn upon his return. And that hope, the dream of that future, in the bright and beautiful wilderness with Dawn, kept him holding on.

∽

August 21, 1782

Dawn swallowed as Mrs. Brooke closed Mr. Taylor's wide staring eyes and stepped away from the bedside. Beside him, his wife began to wail. Tears formed in Dawn's eyes, and she turned away. She started to retreat from the cabin, but her hands were covered in blood. So instead, she huddled around the washbasin with Mrs. Brooke and Mrs. Abbott, scrubbing the stains from her skin.

When finally her hands were clean and dry, Dawn slipped onto the porch. She pulled her blood-stained apron from over her head and crumpled it into a ball, dropping it onto the ground beside her as she sat on the edge of the porch. While Mrs. Taylor's wails drifted through the door, Dawn crossed her arms over her knees and buried her face in them, allowing her own tears to fall.

All day, they had remained pent up inside her. When the first round of militia arrived that morning, she could have been among the many wives that crumpled into hysterics when their husbands were not among the ones to return. Every time stragglers came through the gates, her heart would lift, only to plummet. Still, she had blinked back her tears and remained strong. But no more. She could not stand to keep her hopes up any longer, only to have them dashed time and again.

They had worked to patch up one soldier after another. Lead balls had been retrieved from arms and legs. Another from Mr. McBride's side, above his hip. There had even been a man who had to be sewn up after having removed an arrow from his arm himself. But Mr. Taylor had been the first to arrive, amazingly still alive after taking a bullet to the abdomen. The surgery had proven too difficult, too bloody, though, and he had succumbed to his injuries.

Was that Jacob out there somewhere? Had he taken a ball to the abdomen? Or worse? Did he lie somewhere in a field, with those brown eyes of his wide, unseeing? Or had he attempted to come back to her but died somewhere along the way? Daniel Boone had arrived with the first group, and with a short list of names of those who had died en route to the fort. Jacob's name was not on the list. But that did not mean that he was not dead. Her last ounce of hope had run out, like the sand in an hourglass.

Mrs. Abbott came out onto the porch. She sat beside Dawn and rubbed her back. "This is no easy task, even when your own heart is not grieving."

Dawn shook her head. "I cannot do it anymore."

"I know, dear. I know. Come and eat something. Remember the stew Rebecca had simmering over the fire before we left."

Dawn nearly retched. She shook her head again. "I cannot eat. I...I just want to be alone."

"Let us get you home, then." Mrs. Abbott placed a hand

under her arm and helped her from her seat. The Taylors' cabin was across the way, near the far end of the fort, so it seemed to take forever to make the journey at the slow pace with which her feet moved. From inside several cabins, crying could be heard. And in others, there was utter silence. Women grieved or were already spent from their grieving.

Finally, they made it to her cabin, and Mrs. Abbott swung the door open. The inside was empty, devoid of people. Dawn entered and crawled onto the bed, pulling her knees up and curling around herself.

"We will keep Mary for the night unless we hear otherwise. Let us know if you need anything, and I mean absolutely anything, before morning." Mrs. Abbott waited in the doorway for her nod before she would leave.

When the door shut, Dawn allowed her tears to flow unchecked. She allowed the inevitable truth to seep into her bones and for the grief to consume her. Jacob was gone. She had only just been reunited with him, with her other half. They had shared only two short months together before he had been ripped from her life. And yet, it felt like so much more.

With Edmund not having returned, either, it would just be her and Mary again. They would have to find a new normal for their lives. One without Jacob's smile or his kindness. Without him there to consider their needs and wants. To kiss her at the end of a long day or to whisk Mary onto his shoulders. Sobs overcame Dawn.

When they finally subsided, sleep tugged at her, and she allowed it to pull her into its dark, comforting abyss.

A loud banging at the door jarred Dawn from her sleep. Her brows gathered as she listened for the sound. "Dawn, come now!" Was that Rebecca's voice? What would Rebecca need so urgently? Had something happened to Mrs. Abbott?

Dawn hastened to the door and swung it open.

Rebecca stood outside. "Two more riders have come in. Ma needs your help."

Dawn's shoulders sagged. How could she do this again? She had nothing left to give of herself. Dusk had fallen, but she looked to the gate where two horses were, as well as several men. It appeared one rider stood beside his mount while the other was laid over the saddle. Was the man even alive?

Dawn pinched the bridge of her nose as she turned back to Rebecca. "Has someone fetched Mrs. Brooke?" The experienced woman had served as a nurse with the Continental Army before following her husband to Bryan's Station. Even after becoming widowed, she continued as the station's nurse in the absence of a physician. Since the siege had ensued a few days prior, her expertise had proved invaluable.

"She was still with Mrs. Taylor, so Ma went to fetch her herself. She told me to come wake you, then go back to keep an eye on the children."

Dawn nodded. "Thank you, Rebecca." She attempted to offer some semblance of a smile before she turned and trudged toward the gate. She had told Mrs. Abbott she could not handle any more. Why had she not sought out another woman to help with the injured? Or asked Rebecca to assist and allowed Ruth to watch over the younger children? Though, with the state the one rider appeared to be in, she may have wanted to save her eldest daughter from the trauma. And there were few women in the fort who had not been impacted in some way by the battle.

So the task at hand fell to her. Dawn crossed her arms as though to warm herself and walked toward the group as the men worked to unload the one man from the saddle. With the care they took, he must still be alive. Dawn quickened her steps.

At the sound of crunching grass behind her, she glanced around to find Mrs. Abbott and Mrs. Brooke dashing toward her. When she turned back, her gaze landed upon the first rider and his mount. Dawn slowed to a stop. It could not be.

Samson's coat seemed darker in dusk, but his coloring was unmistakable, even with his head hung low to the ground in apparent exhaustion. And beside him, even without his waistcoat, she would recognize that man anywhere. For he bore the brown hair and thin build of her husband. "Jacob!" She screamed his name and took off at a run.

CHAPTER 19

A man's heart deviseth his way: but the Lord directeth his steps.

— PROVERBS 16:9

Jacob winced at the pain that ricocheted through his chest as Dawn's body collided with his, but he wrapped his arms around her and buried his face in her hair, breathing in the scent of her and relishing the feel of her body against his. For he had thought he would never feel that sensation again. *Thank You, God, for allowing me to come back to her.*

After a moment, he eased back. As much as he wanted to enjoy Dawn's presence, Edmund's care was more important. "You have no idea how glad I am to see your face again, but our reunion must be postponed." He nodded to where several men had hauled Edmund from his horse and held him by all four limbs.

Dawn gasped. Her hand left Jacob's body and flew to her mouth. "That is…" Her voice cracked.

"Yes. We need to get him inside now. It is bad, Dawn. It is a miracle he is still alive." Jacob whispered the words for only his wife and the two women behind her to hear.

Mrs. Brooke gave Edmund a quick sweep of her eyes before she started issuing orders. "I need somewhere better than a bed to tend to this one. Elijah, how big is the table in your cabin?"

"Big enough. Come." Elijah led the men carrying Edmund to his corner cabin, where Edmund was laid out upon the table. The man groaned when the arrow protruding from his back caught on the edge.

While the men still supported his left side, Mrs. Brooke pulled a sheathed knife from her pocket. "Lamps. I need lamps," she called out as she unsheathed the knife and began sawing at the arrow. As soon as the back was removed, the men slid Edmund farther onto the table. He groaned again. Each pained sound tore at Jacob, but at least they meant that Edmund was still alive.

"I need all the linens and bandages you can find, as much hot water as you can prepare, and I need a sewing kit. I will not have this man dying on my watch if I can help it." Mrs. Brooke's face was set in determination as she cut Edmund's garments from his upper half. Oil lamps had been brought into the room and set on the chairs and bench around them. Still, there was only a low amount of light.

Jacob swallowed.

"Does he have any other injuries besides the arrow?" Mrs. Brooke turned her attention to him.

Jacob dipped his chin. "After taking the arrow, he fell from his horse and was trampled."

Mrs. Brooke's eyes widened before she swept her gaze over Edmund's body again. She whispered a string of words, likely a prayer. Then she leaned against the table, gripping it in her fingers so that the knuckles turned white. "How long ago?" Her voice was much quieter now than when she had barked orders.

"The battle happened early in the morning yesterday. Well before noon."

Mrs. Brooke shook her head before she took a deep breath and squared her shoulders. "The arrow must be taken out first. Once that wound has been tended to, I will assess for other injuries." She looked at Dawn and Mrs. Abbott, who both nodded before taking up positions on either side of her.

Jacob stared at Dawn as the lamplight gave her a soft glow. She shared the same emotionally spent but determined expression as Mrs. Brooke. She seemed prepared for whatever may come their way. His precious wife must have been assisting with the injured soldiers as they returned to the fort. How many times had she hoped the face before her would be his? And how many times had she been disappointed? Had she given up hope when dusk cloaked them in darkness? His chest ached.

Mrs. Brooke pulled the arrow from Edmund's abdomen, and blood bubbled up from the wound. Without instruction, Dawn pressed fabric to the wound to staunch the bleeding. When Mrs. Brooke held her knife over her hands, she removed the fabric and pressure long enough for the other woman to widen the wound, then resumed her position. Mrs. Abbott handed Mrs. Brooke a needle and thread, and only then did Dawn back away.

Mrs. Brooke slid her fingers inside Edmund's rent flesh. First, she stitched the unseen wound inside, then she sewed his skin closed. When the task was complete and no bleeding remained, she stood up straight and took a deep breath.

After washing the blood from her hands, Mrs. Brooke examined the rest of his body for injuries. "It does not appear that he has any broken bones that I can find. We may know more when he wakes. But for now, I have done all I can. We must watch for infection and pray that it does not set up." She pulled a quilt over his body before she settled in the chair beside him. "I will take first watch."

Mrs. Abbott washed her hands, then squeezed Mrs. Brooke's shoulder. "Send Mrs. Craig for me if you need anything before I come to relieve you."

Mrs. Brooke offered her a weary smile.

Mrs. Abbott came across the room and embraced him. "I am so thankful for your return." She pulled back and gripped his shoulders. "Mary is at my cabin. You and Dawn may fetch her whenever you are ready, but she is welcome to stay as long as you need."

Jacob inclined his head as the woman slipped out the door. While Dawn washed the blood from her hands, he moved over to Edmund's side. *God, You have shown me what is truly important in life. People. Family. Not what one accomplishes. Please allow this man the same opportunity.* Mrs. Brooke's worried and weary, lined face, reminded him of Edmund's comment about her beauty. Perhaps if he were to pull through, he could find happiness with this widow who seemed to care more deeply about him than simply a nurse to a patient.

Dawn appeared at his side and took his hand. Silently, she inclined her head toward the door. Jacob followed her out into the night, where finally a cool breeze filtered through the fort.

Once outside, Dawn wrapped her arms around his middle and nestled her head into his chest. "I thought I had lost you," she whispered.

"I thought I was lost to you as well." Jacob held her close and laid his cheek upon her head. "I never should have left you and Mary. I am so sorry. Can you ever forgive me?"

Dawn looked up at him with tear-filled eyes. "Forgive you? Of course. How could I ever be mad at you when you came back to me? I do not care what I may have said in the past—I love you, Jacob McFadin, and I hope to never see another day of this life without you in it."

"Oh, Dawn. I love you too." He pressed a kiss to her lips, a kiss filled with the promise of forever. A kiss that said this was only the beginning. Jacob pulled back from her and smiled. "I have a surprise for you."

Her brows pulled together. "A surprise?"

"Edmund asked us to take Mary, to be her parents."

Dawn's mouth dropped open. But then her gaze slid toward the cabin door.

"Not because he was injured," Jacob added. "He asked before we ever went into battle. He said he had been thinking on it for a while."

"Really?" A smile crept onto her face.

Jacob nodded.

"Oh, Jacob. I would love nothing more."

He took her hand into his. "There is one more matter which we need to resolve." Jacob glanced about, then led Dawn a few feet away from the cabin where he was sure no one could overhear. She watched him with her chin angled and brows raised. "Dawn, I wish to make our marriage a true union in every sense of the word. Perhaps not tonight, for my head still aches from where I fell from Samson."

Dawn gasped. "You fell? Are you injured?" She glanced him over, eyes wide in the darkness. Jacob chuckled and caught a knuckle under her chin, coaxing her lovely eyes back to his.

"Only a few aches and pains and a bump to the head. Nothing that will not heal in a day or two."

His wife sighed, and her lips tipped up in a grin before she stepped closer. "Then I would be most glad to make this marriage a true one....when you are better."

Jacob's smile widened. "Then let us go get our girl." Dawn leaned into him as they went to embrace the family God had blessed them with.

August 22, 1782

Dawn peered through the doorway early the next afternoon and grinned. Jacob's chin was settled on his chest above his crossed arms, and soft snores emanated from his body. Meanwhile, Mary played quietly on the floor, pretending her small collection of pinecones was a family. Jacob needed the rest nearly as much as Edmund did, after having ridden all night and day to bring the other man to help. Dawn went to him and pulled a chair up beside him before she gently shook his arm.

Jacob blinked, then abruptly sat up. "I fell asleep." His voice held an edge of panic.

Dawn chuckled. "All is well. Mary is playing safely in the floor. And Edmund is awake."

"He is?"

Dawn nodded, a smile stretching her face.

Jacob wiped his hands on the front of his breeches and stood. "Can we see him?"

Dawn inclined her head again. "Mary, would you like to see your uncle?"

The child's reaction was as quick and pleased as Jacob's. She popped from the ground and nodded before collecting her pinecones and depositing them in the basket in the corner. Then she ran up to Jacob and raised her arms. Jacob winced as he lifted her but did not hesitate to do so. Dawn gave a slight shake of her head.

Together, the three of them walked to Elijah Craig's cabin where Edmund was still stationed. Likely, it would be another day or two before it was safe for him to be moved. Though his waking was a positive sign, he had suffered great trauma, and moving him too soon could prove detrimental.

When they stepped into the room, they stopped, for Edmund appeared to be sleeping once more. Mrs. Brooke offered them a tired smile as she motioned them in. "He is in and out," she whispered. "But you are free to visit."

They approached and sat on the bench. Edmund's face was pale, but his chest rose and fell gently, and no perspiration showed on his brow.

He must have heard their approach, for the turned his head to the side and smiled the smallest of smiles. "'Tis good to see your face without an arrow in my side," Edmund managed to say. "Did you tell them?"

Jacob gave a tilt of his head. "I told Dawn, but not Mary. I wanted to make sure it was what you still wanted."

"I told you." Edmund swallowed. "It had nothing to do with the battle. 'Tis what is best."

Jacob nodded, then turned to Mary. "Mary, dear, Mr. Fairfax, your uncle, he thinks that Dawn and I should be your ma and pa."

Mary's little mouth dropped open. She blinked at Edmund. Then she flashed a bright smile at Dawn and Jacob. "Yes!" She threw her arms around Dawn's neck. After she squeezed her for several moments, she did the same to Jacob. Both he and Dawn chuckled.

Mary slipped from the bench and walked over beside Edmund's head. "T'ank you, Uncle."

"You are welcome, child." Edmund closed his eyes as if he could no longer hold them open.

Dawn reached out and took Mary's hand. "We should let him rest now."

Together, they walked out into the sunshine. Mary skipped ahead of them.

"Want to visit Sarah and Abraham, Mary?" Jacob asked.

Dawn gave him a sideways glance. What did he have up his sleeve?

"Yes!"

"Good. I would like to take your *ma* for a walk." He emphasized the word.

Dawn grinned and leaned into him. It did not matter how hot the day was or how the sun beat down on them, for they were together. And they were family. She would gladly walk to the ends of the earth with them and for them. Plus, perhaps her husband had more than a simple walk in mind, given their conversation the previous afternoon. Dare she to hope?

At Mrs. Abbott's, they shared the good news of Edmund's waking and dropped Mary off to play with the other young children. Then Jacob took Dawn's hand and placed it in the crook of his arm as they began their turn about the fort.

"There is a matter I wanted to discuss with you."

Dawn glanced up at Jacob. "What is that?"

"How do you feel about leaving the fort?"

"Leaving?" She considered the thought for a moment. "Where would we go? Just somewhere safer? To your family?"

Jacob gave her a guilty grin. "Yes. I thought we might join my family in the west. Only, I did not know how you would feel about leaving Mrs. Abbott or taking Mary away from Edmund."

Dawn took a deep breath. "I...I had not considered such."

"You do not have to reply right away. And I want you to feel no pressure to make your decision one way or another."

Dawn nodded, but the question was already rolling around in her mind. Leaving Mrs. Abbott would certainly be difficult as she had come to know the woman as family. And though Edmund had entrusted them with Mary's care, was it right to separate the family members? She would certainly want to discuss the matter with him before they made their final decision.

But to leave this unrest and join Jacob's family? It did sound tempting. After all, they would be gaining another family there. And Dawn had learned just how precious found family was.

CHAPTER 20

> He appointed the moon for seasons: the sun
> knoweth his going down.
>
> — PSALM 104:19

SEPTEMBER 21, 1782

*A*bove Jacob, the stars were tiny pinpoints of white in a black midnight sky above Raccoon Springs. Sleep eluded him, but it could only be attributed to anticipation. As much as he had desired to leave his family and make a name for himself, now he could not wait for their familiar faces. For his mother's warm, accepting embrace and Joseph's optimism and teasing. He could not wait to unite the family that he had grown up with to the family that had found him, the one God had created for him.

He turned to see Dawn's face, barely more than a foot away from his, her eyes closed in a peaceful sleep, with the light of the full moon washing over her beautiful features. How incredible that God had brought her back to him. That

He had blessed Jacob with someone so wonderful, inside and out, as a wife. In contrast to the dark of night that shrouded them, his future seemed brighter than ever with her by his side.

He knew not exactly where they would abide besides near his family. And he knew not how he would provide for Dawn and Mary. But all of that would work itself out—Jacob was sure of it. And he no longer held any hesitation at doing whatever it took, even if it meant following his brothers into business or living in their shadows. For he would not be alone in that shadow.

Pulling a hand from where it had been tucked beneath his head, he pushed a stray lock of soft blond hair from Dawn's face, which had regained its healthy glow. Then he did the same for Mary, who was nestled between them. Her white-blonde hair was even softer than Dawn's, with more curl. In her sleep, it stuck out at all angles.

What a privilege it would be to watch her grow.

Thank You, God, for blessing me with these two. Thank You for bringing Dawn back into my life and keeping us safe and together through these past months.

"So precious." Dawn's whispered words floated to him on the night air.

Jacob opened his eyes and met her smile with one of his own. "Yes, she is," he agreed before he reached across and took Dawn's hand. "You have no idea how grateful I am for the opportunity to be her father. To be your husband."

"I still cannot hardly believe God brought you back to me. You know, I never apologized for disappearing on you."

He gave her hand a reassuring squeeze. "Dawn, it is in the past. God brought us back together. And He will see us through whatever comes next. That is all I need to know. I see that now."

"Me too. Though, I guess I should apologize for making us travel to Bryan's Station at all. I thought things had to be a certain way, and I was wrong. I could have saved us from all of those dangers. All of those close calls."

"We never would have made it here if we did not go through what we have. I believe I would have loved you and Mary, but I do not believe I would have seen how truly important you were to me without the battles we faced. Or have found the peace and contentment that I needed to be able to live this life with you. I am afraid I still would have done something drastic in the end."

His wife shrugged a shoulder. "As hard as it was, God brought us on the journey we had to take, I suppose."

"Yes. And it all started here. Do you remember?"

Dawn smiled. "That night, I knew I recognized your voice. Whatever were you doing in the woods then?"

"Following you. I did not want you to get hurt...even though I did not know it was you."

She laughed. "You scared me instead."

"I suppose I did. What took you into the forest that night?"

"I was foraging for dandelions so Mary and I did not starve."

Jacob shook his head. "I still cannot understand how someone could be as vile as they were to you and Mary. But that was the best day of my life, you know. The day your stepfather cast you out. It was the day God brought you back to me."

Dawn tilted her head with an affectionate smile. "It was a dream come true when He brought you back into my life." Then she frowned. "Only, it was difficult for me to open my heart to that blessing. After the way my stepparents treated me, I no longer believed anyone except my parents, anyone except for blood family, could love me. That is why I was so adamant about taking Mary to her uncle." She sighed. "If only I had known."

Jacob rubbed his thumb over the back of her hand. "I

suppose we were both blind to what was right before us, to the blessing that had been handed to us."

"In many ways, yes."

"At least we were both wise enough to open our eyes."

Dawn chuckled softly. "True." Her gaze fell to Mary. "I could not imagine my life without either of you."

"Me either."

Mary rolled over, her flailing arm landing on top of his. Her little brow furrowed before blue eyes blinked open. "Time to wake?"

Jacob smiled down at her. "No, sweet one. Go back to sleep."

She nodded and nestled closer, curling up against his chest. "Night, Pa," she whispered, so quietly he thought he might have imagined it. But a little gasp came from Dawn's direction, and when he met her gaze, she held a look of pure wonder.

Though Mary had seemed elated to have Jacob and Dawn as her parents, she had yet to call either of them as such. But now, here they were, less than a week into their travels and in her sleepy state, she had given him the best reward she ever could have. Finally, it did not matter what battles he had fought or what accomplishments he held to his name. All that mattered were these moments with the ones he loved, and all the firsts they would share. For nothing could be better than the sense of wholeness that to love and be loved offered.

~

August 29, 1782

"We should be getting close." A wrinkle marred Jacob's brow, and his mouth pinched as he looked from the map to the land around them. The Green River was a day's travel behind them, and the land had begun to level. From where they stood on a rise, they could see for miles and miles. Yet all that greeted his gaze was the green upon green of the tree canopies.

Dawn laid her hand on his arm. "We will find them," she reassured him.

"I never should have strayed. We have acres and acres of land between all four of us. Even if we find the land, they could be anywhere on it."

"As we discussed that night at Raccoon Springs, all happened as it should have, in accordance to God's will. We cannot doubt that. Do you remember at all where they said they might settle?"

Jacob lowered the map and surveyed their surroundings. *God, please lead him*, Dawn silently prayed. Suddenly, the map was up again and Jacob was examining a certain area. He turned to use the saddle as a table and ran his finger along the page. "There was a river. Joseph wants to start a mill. Here." He pointed.

"Then that is where we will go. Right, Mary?" She looked to the child where she sat atop Samson.

The little one nodded, her grin as wide as ever. What a blessing it was that the child was always so willing to travel into the unknown. But perhaps that was the way. After all, they were her parents now. And really, had been all along. Had Dawn not trusted her own parents so wholeheartedly? Did she not trust her heavenly Father so willingly even now?

Dawn grinned and tilted her face heavenward, allowing the warmth of the sunlight to wash over her. *God, lead us.*

When she opened her eyes, a large bird swooped down from above them and veered to the left. As she took in its bright white head and dark-brown body and wings, she gasped. "Do you see that?"

Jacob grunted. "Incredible."

"A bald eagle. *Haliaeetus leucocephalus*." In June, the bald eagle had officially been chosen as the bird for the national seal of the United States of America. For all, it was a symbol of strength and freedom. And it was no wonder, for Dawn had never seen a more majestic animal in all her life.

As quickly as it appeared, it disappeared back into the trees below. Jacob took Samson's reins in hand and held out his other for her to take. This was their favorite way to travel now, she and him hand in hand, with Mary perched tall atop Samson.

Together, they mounted the hill before them, heading down into the valley and one step closer to their future.

～

The sun drifted low over the horizon, nearly lost behind the tree line, and dusk threatened to fall around them. Dawn halted and waited for Jacob's gaze to meet hers. "We need to stop for the night."

Jacob sighed, his shoulders sagging. "You are right. I should not have pushed everyone this long as it is." He glanced to the sliver of orange painting the edge of the sky. "We will be eating the evening meal in the dark."

"We will have the light of the fire. But we do need to eat and rest so we may resume our search tomorrow."

Jacob nodded, then looked around. "There." He motioned to where four large cedars formed a shelter of sorts. He led Samson over, and within the hour, camp was set and salted pork sizzled over the fire. The meat could have easily been eaten without being warmed, but the fire and warm food were a blessing in themselves. Because the threat of attack still loomed when they left Bryan's Station, it was several days before they had been brave enough to risk starting a campfire and alerting anyone around them of their presence.

While Dawn kept the meat from burning, Jacob sat beside her with Mary in his lap, telling of one harrowing experience from when he had served as a messenger in the War of Independence. He exaggerated each tiny detail, and Mary's eyes were wide, her little mouth hanging open as she soaked up every word. Dawn smiled.

A branch cracked out in the blackness of night, drawing their attention. Jacob settled Mary on the ground between him and Dawn and knelt, listening. The sound had come from the opposite direction of where Samson was tied for grazing.

"Who goes there?" A deep voice shouted through the darkness.

Jacob sat up straighter, his hand slipping from the holster at his side. "Jared?"

Footsteps crunched closer until a sizeable man appeared at the edge of the cedars, his head nearly touching the lower limbs as the firelight flickered on his scarred face. His gaze swept over the camp, encompassing each one of them. "Jacob?"

"Yes! Yes! We found you!" Jacob took off across the camp and tackled his brother in a hug. Jared grunted as his brother's body impacted his.

"It appears you have." Jared managed to eek out the words as Jacob squeezed his chest. He stiffly returned his brother's hug, patting his back as he did so. After several moments, he finally pushed at his shoulder. "That is enough, now." Evidently, the eldest brother's demeanor was still as grizzly as it had been when they separated ways.

Jacob stepped back.

"Put out your fire and come along. Ma will be glad to see you all."

Dawn extinguished the flames and kicked dirt over the embers while the men gathered their packs and haphazardly loaded them onto Samson, carrying some instead of taking the time to secure them to the saddle. Despite the darkness surrounding them, their steps were lighter than ever as Jared led them toward their future home.

After about twenty minutes, they stood outside a clearing

which held a log cabin twice the size of the homes at Bryan's Station, as well as a generous plot for herbs and vegetables. A split-rail fence stretched behind the house and garden. "Here, I will put your horse in the corral. You go on in." Jared took Samson and led him around the side of the cabin.

Jacob paused outside the door and took a deep breath, as though he was unsure how his mother would respond.

"Go on," Dawn whispered.

He pushed the door open slowly and stepped in. Dawn and Mary followed, closing the door behind them.

"Jared, can you—" Mrs. McFadin stopped in her tracks as she turned from a washbasin. The towel and the plate in her hand fell to the floor with a clatter. Her face crumpled as tears came to her eyes and her hand went to her mouth.

"Jacob!" Jemimah cheered as she charged toward them, her mending landing in the floor as well. She threw her arms around him in a hug while Jonah and Joseph came over, their jaws hanging open. When Jemimah relinquished Jacob and moved on to Dawn and Mary, Jonah took his turn. Each of the siblings embraced the prodigal son before also sharing a hug with Dawn and Mary.

Joseph even whisked Mary into his arms and twirled her about the room, eliciting girlish giggles. "Mary, you came to see us!"

Finally, Mrs. McFadin approached Jacob slowly, tears glistening on her cheeks. She placed a hand softly on his cheek. "You came back," she whispered.

"I did." Jacob nodded.

Mrs. McFadin wrapped her son in a hug. Her body shook as she shed her silent tears. When she pulled back, she graced him with another smile before turning to Dawn.

"And I brought my family," Jacob added with a proud grin.

Mrs. McFadin hugged Dawn, squeezing her tightly. "I knew God would bring you all back to me. I knew it."

Tears sprang into Dawn's eyes as well, for this woman was not only praising her son's return, but hers and Mary's as well.

When Dawn had doubted that a single person could love her, that anyone could love Mary except for a blood relative, here was all the love in the world waiting for them. Not only did the connection flow between Dawn and Jacob and Mary, but it spread to Mrs. McFadin and Jacob's brothers and sister as well, as expansive as the star-speckled sky outside the cabin. Never again would she or Mary want for love.

Did you enjoy this book? We hope so!
Would you take a quick minute to leave a review where you purchased the book?
It doesn't have to be long. Just a sentence or two telling what you liked about the story!

~

Love Christian Historical Romance?
Looking for your next favorite book?
Become a Wild Heart Books insider and receive a FREE ebook and get exclusive updates on new releases before anyone else.
Sign up for our newsletter now.
https://wildheartbooks.org/newsletter

AUTHOR'S NOTE

Thank you so much for joining me for this new series and for Jacob and Dawn's journey. I pray you adored their story, as well as getting to know sweet little Mary. There will be more to come of the McFadin family, so please join us on Facebook in The Reader's Nest to stay tuned for further releases.

In this novel, I attempted to show a bit about what a bountiful and diverse land Kentucky would have been when it was first being settled. Many people, including those who are Kentucky born and raised, are unaware that mountain lions, bears, and wolves were all native to the state at one time and were crowded out as people pressed westward. And though some of us still see animals such as deer and turkey on a regular basis, sometimes daily during certain times of the year, the numbers of all the fish and wildlife our wonderful land once carried have greatly diminished through the years. In doing my research, it was disturbing to see this progression.

However, I thoroughly enjoyed creating a character that appreciated nature as much as I do. (Although I cannot give the scientific names as readily as she does.) For the sake of the novel, I did take some liberties on the timelines of when these

AUTHOR'S NOTE

plants and animals received their scientific names and when they would have become common knowledge to enthusiasts such as Dawn and her father. It is a delicate balance in finding what would be native to the area, would be blooming at the time the story takes place, and had received a published scientific name. So while some of these plants and animals had indeed received their scientific names in 1782 and it had been published, some had received their name but it had yet to be published, and some had yet to receive their scientific name in 1782.

Beyond incorporating native plants and animals into this novel, I did also highlight a couple of pieces of true history within its pages. The Siege of Bryan's Station and the Battle of Blue Licks were real battles that occurred on the dates on which they occurred in the novel. I did try to keep these battles as true to history as possible, though some details were different from report to report, requiring certain information to be left unspecified or to become works of fiction. One such example was when Daniel Boone cautioned the men at the fort against pursuing the enemy. Some more detailed accounts state that he only cautioned them after they were on the pursuit and realized the trail left by the retreating militia was much too obvious. However, he did still go into battle with his fellow soldiers, despite his hesitations, as he did in the novel.

In short, the fort was indeed surrounded by hundreds of Native Americans and British who laid in wait before attacking. The courageous women did indeed travel to the spring despite the looming danger, and a monument now stands in their honor, placed there by the Daughters of the American Revolution. These incredible women were the initial inspiration for this novel.

After their act of bravery, a siege ensued for two days before the enemy retreated. It is reported that Daniel Boone did caution the men not to pursue, but a group of more than one

AUTHOR'S NOTE

hundred did. This resulted in the Battle of Blue Licks, where they suffered heavy losses in a brief battle.

As always, I pray this novel serves to honor those that came before and settled this land and sparks interest in readers in these pieces of history. Please do not forget to leave your review of this novel, and I hope you will join us for Jared's love story next!

DISCUSSION QUESTIONS

1. Life on the Kentucky frontier was perilous, with countless dangers. If you were traveling into the area at the time, what would have worried you the most? How would you have relied on your faith to help you overcome these fears?
2. Jacob and Dawn both had their reasons for leaving the relative safety of the East and traveling beyond the Cumberland Gap. What do you think are some of the various reasons that hundreds of others made the journey into Kentucky?
3. Dawn's father taught her to see God's hand in the world around her. This is a tool she uses throughout her life to reconnect with her heavenly Father and lift her spirits. What methods or tools do you use when you need to feel God's closeness?
4. Despite having loving parents throughout her childhood and preteen years, the abuse and judgment served by her stepfather completely altered Dawn's belief systems and the way that she perceived herself. Have you ever experienced similar

DISCUSSION QUESTIONS

trauma? Can you share how you overcome it or are still working to overcome it? How can we, as Christians, help stop the cycle of abuse and trauma?

5. Jacob feels an inherent need to "make something of himself" and prove himself worthy as a man and husband. Many people today experience similar struggles, feeling sensations of unworthiness because their lives do not look like those of others. Do you believe that this is a flaw that spans across centuries and generations? Have humans always felt the need to fit in and have standing within their communities? How can we overcome this in our own lives?

6. The Cumberland Gap was not widened and opened to wagons until 1796, so families had to travel on foot or horseback. A well-trained, well-built horse like Samson would have been an absolute blessing. How do you think his presence altered the course of the story? Have you ever had a horse or animal that has made a difference in your life? Also, can you imagine walking such distances?

7. In the story, Jacob and Dawn have to make multiple decisions about where to live—separating from Jacob's family to pursue Mary's uncle, choosing to stay at Bryan's Station for a short while, and ultimately, returning to the McFadin lands. What did you think of these decisions?

8. Jacob chooses to pursue those who attacked Bryan's Station but quickly regrets his decision. Often, hindsight provides clarity and shows us what is at stake. Have you ever made a decision that you regretted? How did you learn from it?

9. Family is an important theme throughout the book, both in the sense of blood relatives and found

DISCUSSION QUESTIONS

family. How important is family to you? Can found family members, those unrelated to us, be just as important?

10. In general, what parts of the story struck you or stayed with you the most? Did you learn any new facts?

ABOUT THE AUTHOR

Andrea Byrd is a small-town wife and mom from southern Kentucky who harbors a deep love of days gone by, expressed with pioneer skirts and a once-in-a-lifetime ride in an authentic biplane. She seeks to respect the past, giving voice to those that came before, while reminding readers that no aspect of their past defines them.

Want more?

If you love historical romance, check out the other Wild Heart books!

Rescue in the Wilderness by Andrea Byrd

William Cole cannot forget the cruel burden he carries, not with the pock marks that serve as an outward reminder. Riddled with guilt, he assumed the solitary life of a long hunter, traveling into the wilds of Kentucky each year. But his quiet existence is changed in an instant when, sitting in a tavern, he overhears a man offering his daughter—and her virtue—to the winner of the next round of cards. William's integrity and desire for redemption will not allow him to sit idly by while such an injustice occurs.

Lucinda Gillespie has suffered from an inexplicable illness her entire life. Her father, embarrassed by her condition, has subjected her to a lonely existence of abuse and confinement. But faced with the ultimate betrayal on the eve of her eighteenth birthday, Lucinda quickly realizes her trust is better placed in his hands of the mysterious man who appears at her door. Especially when he offers her the one thing she never thought would be within her grasp—freedom.

In the blink of an eye, both lives change as they begin the difficult, danger-fraught journey westward on the Wilderness Trail. But can they overcome their own perceptions of themselves to find love and the life God created them for?

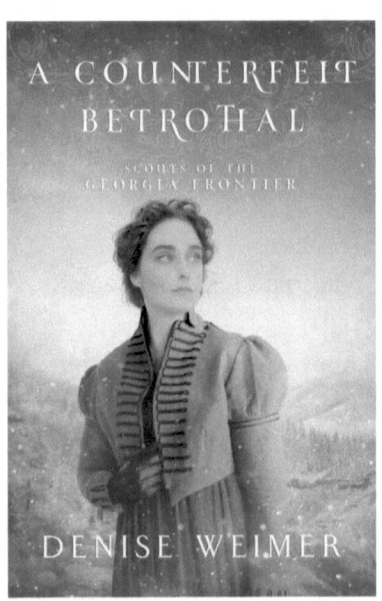

A Counterfeit Betrothal by Denise Weimer

A frontier scout, a healing widow, and a desperate fight for peace.

At the farthest Georgia outpost this side of hostile Creek Territory in 1813, Jared Lockridge serves his country as a scout to redeem his father's botched heritage. If he can help secure peace against Indians allied to the British, he can bring his betrothed to the home he's building and open his cabinetry shop. Then he comes across a burning cabin and a traumatized woman just widowed by a fatal shot.

Freed from a cruel marriage, Esther Andrews agrees to winter at the Lockridge homestead to help Jared's pregnant sister-in-law. Lame in one foot, Esther has always known she is second-hand goods, but the gentle carpenter-turned-scout draws her heart with as much skill as he creates furniture from wood. His family's love offers hope even as violence erupts along the frontier—and Jared's investigation into local incidents brings danger to their doorstep. Yet how could Esther ever hope a loyal man like Jared would choose her over a fine lady?

~

Waltz in the Wilderness by Kathleen Denly

She's desperate to find her missing father. His conscience demands he risk all to help.

Eliza Brooks is haunted by her role in her mother's death, so she'll do anything to find her missing pa—even if it means sneaking aboard a southbound ship. When those meant to protect her abandon and betray her instead, a family friend's unexpected assistance is a blessing she can't refuse.

Daniel Clarke came to California to make his fortune, and a stable job as a San Francisco carpenter has earned him more than most have scraped from the local goldfields. But it's been four years since he left Massachusetts and his fiancé is impatient for his return. Bound for home at last, Daniel Clarke finds his heart and plans challenged by a tenacious young woman with haunted eyes. Though every word he utters seems to offend her, he is determined to see her safely returned to her father. Even if that means risking his fragile engagement.

When disaster befalls them in the remote wilderness of the Southern California mountains, true feelings are revealed, and both must face heart-rending decisions. But how to decide when every choice before them leads to someone getting hurt?

www.ingramcontent.com/pod-product-compliance
Lightning Source LLC
LaVergne TN
LVHW040056080526
838202LV00045B/3660